THE COUNCIL OF JUSTICE

There are crimes for which no punishment is adequate, offences that the written law cannot efface. Herein lies the justification for The Council of Justice — a meeting of great and passionless intellects. These men are indifferent to world opinion. They relentlessly wage their wits and cunning against powerful underworld organisations, against past masters of villainy and against minds equally astute. And to breakers of the unwritten laws they deal death . . .

D1390965

Books by Edgar Wallace
Published by The House of Ulverscroft:

THE AVENGER
WHITE FACE
THE JUST MEN OF CORDOVA

EDGAR WALLACE

THE COUNCIL OF JUSTICE

Complete and Unabridged

ULVERSCROFT
Leicester

First published in Great Britain in 1908

This Large Print Edition
published 2012

British Library CIP Data

Wallace, Edgar, *1875 – 1932*.
  The council of justice.
  1. Detective and mystery stories.
  2. Large type books.
  I. Title
  823.9'12–dc23

ISBN 978–1–4448–0960–2

Published by
F. A. Thorpe (Publishing)
Anstey, Leicestershire

Set by Words & Graphics Ltd.
Anstey, Leicestershire
Printed and bound in Great Britain by
T. J. International Ltd., Padstow, Cornwall

This book is printed on acid-free paper

1

The Red Hundred

It is not for you or me to judge Manfred and his works. I say Manfred, though I might as well have said Gonsalez, or for the matter of that Poiccart, since they are equally guilty or great according to the light in which you view their acts. The most lawless of us would hesitate to defend them, but the greater humanitarian could scarcely condemn them.

From the standpoint of us, who live within the law, going about our business in conformity with the code, and unquestioningly keeping to the left or to the right as the police direct, their methods were terrible, indefensible, revolting.

It does not greatly affect the issue that, for want of a better word, we call them criminals. Such would be mankind's unanimous designation, but I think — indeed, I know — that they were indifferent to the opinions of the human race. I doubt very much whether they expected posterity to honour them.

Their action towards the cabinet minister was murder, pure and simple. Yet, in view of the large humanitarian problems involved, who would describe it as pernicious?

Frankly I say of the three men who killed Sir Philip Ramon, and who slew ruthlessly in the name of Justice, that my sympathies are with them. There are crimes for which there is no adequate punishment, and offences that the machinery of the written law cannot efface. Therein lies the justification for the Four Just Men — the Council of Justice as they presently came to call themselves a council of great intellects, passionless.

And not long after the death of Sir Philip and while England still rang with that exploit, they performed an act or a series of acts that won not alone from the Government of Great Britain, but from the Governments of Europe, a sort of unofficial approval and Falmouth had his wish. For here they waged war against great world-criminals — they pitted their strength, their cunning, and their wonderful intellects against the most powerful organization of the underworld — against past masters of villainous arts, and brains equally agile.

It was the day of days for the Red Hundred. The wonderful inter-national congress was meeting in London, the first great congress of recognized Anarchism. This was no hole-and-corner gathering of hurried men speaking furtively, but one open and unafraid with three policemen specially retained for duty outside the hall, a commissionaire to take tickets at the outer lobby, and a shorthand writer with a knowledge of French and Yiddish to make notes of remarkable utterances.

The wonderful congress was a fact. When it had been broached there were people who laughed at the idea; Niloff of Vitebsk was one because he did not think such openness possible. But little Peter (his preposterous name was Konoplanikova, and he was a reporter on the staff of the foolish *Russkoye Znamza*), this little Peter who had thought out the whole thing, whose idea it was to gather a conference of the Red Hundred in London, who hired the hall and issued the bills (bearing in the top left-hand corner the inverted triangle of the Hundred) asking those Russians in London interested in the building of a Russian Sailors' Home to apply for tickets, who, too, secured a hall where interruption was impossible, was happy — yea, little brothers, it was a great day for Peter.

'You can always deceive the police,' said little Peter enthusiastically; 'call a meeting with a philanthropic object and — *voila!*'

Wrote Inspector Falmouth to the assistant commissioner of police:

Your respected communication to hand. The meeting to be held tonight at the Phoenix Hall, Middlesex Street, E., with the object of raising funds for a Russian Sailors' Home is, of course, the first international congress of the Red Hundred. Shall not be able to get a man inside, but do not think that matters much, as meeting will be engaged throwing flowers at one another and serious business will not commence till the meeting of the inner committee. I enclose a list of men already arrived in London, and have the honour to request that you will send me portraits of undermentioned men.

★ ★ ★

There were three delegates from Baden, Herr Schmidt from Frieburg, Herr Bleaumeau from Karlsruhe, and Herr Von Dunop from Mannheim. They were not considerable persons, even in the eyes of the world of Anarchism; they called for no particular notice, and therefore the strange thing that happened to them on the night of the congress is all the more remarkable.

Herr Schmidt had left his pension in Bloomsbury and was hurrying eastward. It was a late autumn evening and a chilly rain fell, and Herr Schmidt was debating in his mind whether he should go direct to the rendezvous where he had promised to meet his two compatriots, or whether he should call a taxi and drive direct to the hall, when a hand grasped his arm. He turned quickly and reached for his hip pocket. Two men stood behind him and but for themselves the square through which he was passing was deserted.

Before he could grasp the Browning pistol, his other arm was seized and the taller of the two men spoke.

'You are Augustus Schmidt?' he asked.

'That is my name.'

'You are an anarchist?'

'That is my affair.'

'You are at present on your way to a meeting of the Red Hundred?'

Herr Schmidt opened his eyes in genuine astonishment.

'How did you know that?' he asked.

'I am Detective Simpson from Scotland Yard, and I shall take you into custody,' was the quiet reply.

'On what charge?' demanded the German.

'As to that I shall tell you later.'

The man from Baden shrugged his shoulders.

'I have yet to learn that it is an offence in

England to hold opinions.'

A closed motor-car entered the square, and the shorter of the two whistled and the chauffeur drew up near the group.

The anarchist turned to the man who had arrested him.

'I warn you that you shall answer for this,' he said wrathfully. 'I have an important engagement that you have made me miss through your foolery and — '

'Get in!' interrupted the tall man tersely.

Schmidt stepped into the car and the door snapped behind him.

He was alone and in darkness. The car moved on and then Schmidt discovered that there were no windows to the vehicle. A wild idea came to him that he might escape. He tried the door of the car; it was immovable. He cautiously tapped it. It was lined with thin sheets of steel.

'A prison on wheels,' he muttered with a curse, and sank back into the corner of the car.

He did not know London; he had not the slightest idea where he was going. For ten minutes the car moved along. He was puzzled. These policemen had taken nothing from him, he still retained his pistol. They had not even attempted to search him for compromising documents. Not that he had any except the pass for the conference and — the Inner Code!

Heavens! He must destroy that. He thrust his hand into the inner pocket of his coat. It was empty. The thin leather case was gone! His face went grey, for the Red Hundred is no fanciful secret society but a bloody-minded organization with less mercy for bungling brethren than for its sworn enemies. In the thick darkness of the car his nervous fingers groped through all his pockets. There was no doubt at all — the papers had gone.

In the midst of his search the car stopped. He slipped the flat pistol from his pocket. His position was desperate and he was not the kind of man to shirk a risk.

Once there was a brother of the Red Hundred who sold a password to the Secret Police. And the brother escaped from Russia. There was a woman in it, and the story is a mean little story that is hardly worth the telling. Only, the man and the woman escaped, and went to Baden, and Schmidt recognized them from the portraits he had received from headquarters, and one night . . . You understand that there was nothing clever or neat about it. English newspapers would have described it as a 'revolting murder', because the details of the crime were rather shocking. The thing that stood to Schmidt's credit in the books of the Society was that the murderer was undiscovered.

The memory of this episode came back to the anarchist as the car stopped — perhaps this was the thing the police had discovered? Out of the dark corners of his mind came the scene again, and the voice of the man . . . 'Don't! don't! O Christ! don't!' and Schmidt sweated . . .

The door of the car opened and he slipped back the cover of his pistol.

'Don't shoot,' said a quiet voice in the gloom outside, 'here are some friends of yours.'

He lowered his pistol, for his quick ears detected a wheezing cough.

'Von Dunop!' he cried in astonishment.

'And Herr Bleaumeau,' said the same voice. 'Get in, you two.'

Two men stumbled into the car, one dumbfounded and silent — save for the wheezing cough — the other blasphemous and voluble.

'Wait, my friend!' raved the bulk of Bleaumeau; 'Wait! I will make you sorry.'

The door shut and the car moved on.

The two men outside watched the vehicle with its unhappy passengers disappear round a corner and then walked slowly away.

'Extraordinary men,' said the taller.

'Most,' replied the other, and then, 'Von Dunop — isn't he — ?'

'The man who threw the bomb at the Swiss President — yes.'

The shorter man smiled in the darkness.

'Given a conscience, he is enduring his hour,' he said.

The pair walked on in silence and turned into Oxford Street as the clock of a church struck eight.

The tall man lifted his walking-stick and a sauntering taxi pulled up at the curb.

'Aldgate,' he said, and the two men took their seats.

Not until the taxi was spinning along Newgate Street did either of the men speak, and then the shorter asked:

'You are thinking about the woman?'

The other nodded and his companion relapsed into silence; then he spoke again:

'She is a problem and a difficulty, in a way — yet she is the most dangerous of the lot. And the curious thing about it is that if she were not beautiful and young she would not be a problem at all. We're very human, George. God made us illogical that the minor businesses of life should not interfere with the great scheme. And the great scheme is that animal men should select animal women for the mothers of their children.'

9

'*Venenum in auro bibitur,*' the other quoted, which shows that he was an extraordinary detective, 'and so far as I am concerned it matters little to me whether an irresponsible homicide is a beautiful woman or a misshapen negro.'

They dismissed the taxi at Aldgate Station and turned into Middlesex Street.

The meeting-place of the great congress was a hall which was originally erected by an enthusiastic Christian gentleman with a weakness for the conversion of Jews to the New Presbyterian Church. With this laudable object it had been opened with great pomp and the singing of anthems and the enthusiastic proselytizer had spoken on that occasion two hours and forty minutes by the clock.

After twelve months' labour the Christian gentleman discovered that the advantages of Christianity only appeal to very rich Jews indeed, to the Cohens who become Cowans, to the Isaacs who become Grahames, and to the curious low-down Jews who stand in the same relation to their brethren as White Kaffirs to a European community.

So the hall passed from hand to hand, and, failing to obtain a music and dancing licence, went back to the mission-hall stage.

Successive generations of small boys had

destroyed its windows and beplastered its walls. Successive fly-posters had touched its blank face with colour. Tonight there was nothing to suggest that there was any business of extraordinary importance being transacted within its walls. A Russian or a Yiddish or any kind of reunion does not greatly excite Middlesex Street, and had little Peter boldly announced that the congress of the Red Hundred were to meet in full session there would have been no local excitement and — if the truth be told — he might still have secured the services of his three policemen and commissionaire.

To this worthy, a neat, cleanly gentleman in uniform, wearing on his breast the medals for the relief of Chitral and the Sudan Campaigns, the two men delivered the perforated halves of their tickets and passed through the outer lobby into a small room. By a door at the other end stood a thin man with a straggling beard. His eyes were red-rimmed and weak, he wore long narrow buttoned boots, and he had a trick of pecking his head forwards and sideways like an inquisitive hen.

'You have the word, brothers?' he asked, speaking German like one unaccustomed to the language.

The taller of the two strangers shot a swift glance at the sentinel that absorbed the

11

questioner from his cracked patent leather boots to his flamboyant watch-chain. Then he answered in Italian:

'Nothing!'

The face of the guardian flushed with pleasure at the familiar tongue.

'Pass, brother; it is very good to hear that language.'

The air of the crowded hall struck the two men in the face like the blast from a destructor. It was unclean; unhealthy — the scent of an early-morning doss-house.

The hall was packed, the windows were closed and curtained, and as a precautionary measure, little Peter had placed thick blankets before the ventilators.

At one end of the hall was a platform on which stood a semicircle of chairs and in the centre was a table draped with red. On the wall behind the chairs — every one of which was occupied — was a huge red flag bearing in the centre a great white 'C'. It had been tacked to the wall, but one corner had broken away revealing a part of the painted scroll of the mission workers: . . . are the meek, for they shall inherit the earth.

The two intruders pushed their way through a group that were gathered at the door. Three aisles ran the length of the building, and they made their way along the central gangway and found seats near the platform.

A brother was speaking. He was a good and zealous worker but a bad orator. He spoke in German and enunciated commonplaces with hoarse emphasis. He said all the things that other men had said and forgotten. 'This is the time to strike' was his most notable sentence, and notable only because it evoked a faint buzz of applause.

The audience stirred impatiently. The good Bentvitch had spoken beyond his allotted time; and there were other people to speak — and prosy at that. And it would be ten o'clock before the Woman of Gratz would rise.

The babble was greatest in the corner of the hall, where little Peter, all eyes and startled eyebrows, was talking to an audience of his own.

'It is impossible, it is absurd, it is most foolish!' his thin voice rose almost to a scream. 'I should laugh at it — we should all laugh, but the Woman of Gratz has taken the matter seriously, and she is afraid!'

'Afraid!'

'Nonsense!'

'Oh, Peter, the fool!'

There were other things said because everybody in the vicinity expressed an opinion. Peter was distressed, but not by the epithets. He was crushed, humiliated, beaten by his tremendous tidings. He was nearly crying at the horrible thought. The Woman of Gratz was afraid! The Woman of Gratz who . . . It was unthinkable.

He turned his eyes toward the platform, but she was not there.

'Tell us about it, Peter,' pleaded a dozen voices; but the little man with the tears twinkling on his fair eyelashes waved them off.

So far from his incoherent outburst they had learnt only this — that the Woman of Gratz was afraid.

And that was bad enough.

For this woman — she was a girl really, a slip of a child who should have been finishing her education somewhere in Germany — this same woman had once risen and electrified the world.

There had been a meeting in a small Hungarian town to discuss ways and means. And when the men had finished their denunciation of Austria, she rose and talked. A short-skirted little girl with two long flaxen braids of hair, thin-legged, flat-chested, angular, hipless — that is what the men of Gratz noticed as they smiled behind their hands and wondered why her father had brought her to the meeting.

But her speech ... two hours she spoke and no man stirred. A little flat-chested girl full of sonorous phrases — mostly she had collected them from the talk in Old Joseph's kitchen. But with some power of her own, she had spun them together, these inconsiderable truisms, and had endowed them with a wondrous vitality.

They were old, old platitudes, if the truth be told, but at some time in the history of revolution, some long dead genius had coined them, and newly fashioned in the furnace of his soul they had shaped men's minds and directed their great and dreadful deeds.

So the Woman of Gratz arrived, and they talked about her and circulated her speeches in every language. And she grew. The hollow face of this lank girl filled, and the flat bosom rounded and there came softer lines and curves to her angular figure, and, almost before they realized the fact, she was beautiful.

So her fame had grown until her father died and she went to Russia. Then came a series of outrages which may be categorically and briefly set forth:

1: General Maloff shot dead by an unknown woman in his private room at the Police Bureau, Moscow.

2: Prince Hazallarkoff shot dead by an unknown woman in the streets of Petrograd.

3: Colonel Kaverdavskov killed by a bomb thrown by a woman who made her escape.

And the Woman of Gratz leapt to a greater fame. She had been arrested half a dozen times, and whipped twice, but they could prove nothing against her and elicit nothing from her — and she was very beautiful.

Now to the thundering applause of the waiting delegates, she stepped upon the platform and took the last speaker's place by the side of the red-covered table.

She raised her hand and absolute and complete silence fell on the hall, so much so that her first words sounded strident and shrill, for she had attuned her voice to the din. She recovered her pitch and dropped her voice to a conversational tone.

She stood easily with her hands clasped behind her and made no gesture. The emotion that was within her she conveyed through her wonderful voice. Indeed, the power of the speech lay rather in its delivery than in its substance, for only now and then did she depart from the unwritten text of Anarchism: the right of the oppressed to overthrow the oppressor; the divinity of violence; the sacredness of sacrifice and martyrdom in the cause of enlightenment.

One phrase alone stood apart from the commonplace of her oratory. She was speaking of the Theorists who counsel reform and condemn violence, 'These Christs who deputize their Calvaries,' she called them with fine scorn, and the hall roared its approval of the imagery.

It was the fury of the applause that disconcerted her; the taller of the two men who sat watching her realized that much. For when the shouting had died down and she strove to resume, she faltered and stammered and then was silent. Then abruptly and with surprising vehemence she began again. But she had changed the direction of her oratory, and it was upon another subject that she now spoke. A subject nearer to her at that moment than any other, for her pale cheeks flushed and a feverish light came to her eyes as she spoke.

' ... and now, with all our perfect organization, with the world almost within our grasp — there comes somebody who says *Stop!* — and we who by our acts have terrorized kings and dominated the councils of empires, are ourselves threatened!'

The audience grew deadly silent. They were silent before, but now the silence was painful.

The two men who watched her stirred a

little uneasily, as though something in her speech had jarred. Indeed, the suggestion of braggadocio in her assertion of the Red Hundred's power had struck a discordant note.

The girl continued speaking rapidly.

'We have heard — you have heard — we know of these men who have written to us. They say' — her voice rose — 'that we shall not do what we do. They threaten us — they threaten me — that we must change our methods, or they will punish as — as we — punish; kill as we kill — ' There was a murmuring in the audience and men looked at one another in amazement. For terror unmistakable and undisguised was written on her pale face and shone from those wondrous eyes of hers. 'But we will defy — '

Loud voices and the sound of scuffling in the little anteroom interrupted her, and a warning word shouted brought the audience to its feet.

'The police!'

A hundred stealthy hands reached for cunning pockets, but somebody leapt upon a bench, near the entrance, and held up an authoritative hand.

'Gentlemen, there is no occasion for alarm — I am Detective-Superintendent Falmouth from Scotland Yard, and I have no quarrel with the Red Hundred.'

Little Peter, transfixed for the moment, pushed his way towards the detective.

'Who do you want — what do you want?' he asked.

The detective stood with his back to the door and answered.

'I want two men who were seen to enter this hall: two members of an organization that is outside the Red Hundred. They — '

'Ha!' The woman who still stood upon the platform leant forward with blazing eyes.

'I know — I know!' she cried breathlessly; 'the men who threatened us — who threatened me — The Four Just Men!'

2

The Fourth Man

The tall man's hand was in his pocket when the detective spoke.

When he had entered the hall he had thrown a swift glance round the place and taken in every detail. He had seen the beaded strip of unpainted wood which guarded the electric light cables, and had improved the opportunity whilst the prosy brother was speaking to make a further reconnaissance. There was a white porcelain switchboard with half a dozen switches at the left-hand side of the platform. He judged the distance and threw up the hand that held the pistol.

Bang! Bang!

A crash of broken glass, a quick flash of blue flame from the shattered fuses — and the hall was in darkness. It happened before the detective could spring from his form into the yelling, screaming crowd — before the police officer could get a glance at the man who fired the shots.

In an instant the place was a pandemonium.

'Silence!' Falmouth roared above the din; 'Silence! Keep quiet, you miserable cowards — show a light here, Brown, Curtis — Inspector, where are your men's lanterns!' The rays of a dozen bull's-eye lamps waved over the struggling throng. 'Open your lanterns' — and to the seething mob, 'Silence!'

Then a bright young officer remembered that he had seen gasbrackets in the room, and struggled through the howling mob till he came to the wall and found the gas-fitting with his lantern. He struck a match and lit the gas, and the panic subsided as suddenly as it had begun.

Falmouth, choked with rage, threw his eye round the hall.

'Guard the door,' he said briefly; 'the hall is surrounded and they cannot possibly escape.'

He strode swiftly along the central aisle, followed by two of his men, and with an agile leap, sprang on to the platform and faced the audience. The Woman of Gratz, with a white set face, stood motionless, one hand resting on the little table, the other at her throat. Falmouth raised his hand to enjoin silence and the lawbreakers obeyed.

'I have no quarrel with the Red Hundred,' he said. 'By the law of this country it is permissible to hold opinions and propagate doctrines, however objectionable they be — I am here to arrest two men who have broken the laws of this country. Two persons who are part of the organization known as the Four Just Men.'

All the time he was speaking his eyes searched the faces before him. He knew that one-half of the audience could not understand him and that the hum of talk that arose as he finished was his speech in course of translation.

The faces he sought he could not discern. To be exact, he hoped that his scrutiny would induce two men, of whose identity he was ignorant, to betray themselves.

There are little events, unimportant in themselves, which occasionally lead to tremendous issues. A skidding motor-bus that crashed into a private car in Piccadilly had led to the discovery that there were three vociferous foreign gentlemen imprisoned in the overturned vehicle. It led to the further discovery that the chauffeur had disappeared in the confusion of the collision. In the darkness, comparing notes, the three prisoners had arrived at a conclusion — to wit, that their abduction was a sequel to a mysterious letter each had received, which bore the signature 'The Four Just Men'.

So in the panic occasioned by the accident, they were sufficiently indiscreet to curse the

Four Just Men by name, and, the Four Just Men being a sore topic with the police, they were questioned further, and the end of it was that Superintendent Falmouth motored eastward in great haste and was met in Middlesex Street by a reserve of police specially summoned.

He was at the same disadvantage he had always been — the Four Just Men were to him names only, symbols of a swift remorseless force that struck surely and to the minute — and nothing more.

Two or three of the leaders of the Red Hundred had singled themselves out and drew closer to the platform.

'We are not aware,' said Francois, the Frenchman, speaking for his companions in faultless English, 'we are not aware of the identity of the men you seek, but on the understanding that they are not brethren of our Society, and moreover' — he was at a loss for words to put the fantastic situation — 'and moreover since they have threatened us — threatened us,' he repeated in bewilderment, 'we will afford you every assistance.'

The detective jumped at the opportunity.

'Good!' he said and formed a rapid plan.

The two men could not have escaped from the hall. There was a little door near the platform, he had seen that — as the two men he sought had seen it. Escape seemed possible through there; they had thought so, too. But Falmouth knew that the outer door leading from the little vestibule was guarded by two policemen. This was the sum of the discovery made also by the two men he sought. He spoke rapidly to Francois.

'I want every person in the hall to be vouched for,' he said quickly. 'Somebody must identify every man, and the identifier must himself be identified.'

The arrangements were made with lightning-like rapidity. From the platform in French, German and Yiddish, the leaders of the Red Hundred explained the plan. Then the police formed a line, and one by one the people came forward, and shyly, suspiciously or self-consciously, according to their several natures, they passed the police line.

'That is Simon Czech of Buda-Pest.'

'Who identifies him?'

'I.' — a dozen voices.

'Pass.'

'This is Michael Ranekov of Odessa.'

'Who identifies him?'

'I,' said a burly man, speaking in German.

'And you?'

There was a little titter, for Michael is the best-known man in the order. Some there were who, having passed the line, waited to identify their kinsfolk and fellow-countrymen.

'It seems much simpler than I could have imagined.'

It was the tall man with the trim beard, who spoke in a guttural tone which was neither German nor Yiddish. He was watching with amused interest the examination.

'Separating the lambs from the goats with a vengeance,' he said with a faint smile, and his taciturn companion nodded. Then he asked — 'Do you think any of these people will recognize you as the man who fired?'

The tall man shook his head decisively.

'Their eyes were on the police — and besides I am too quick a shot. Nobody saw me unless — '

'The Woman of Gratz?' asked the other, without showing the slightest concern.

'The Woman of Gratz,' said George Manfred.

They formed part of a struggling line that moved slowly toward the police barrier.

'I fear,' said Manfred, 'that we shall be forced to make our escape in a perfectly obvious way — the bull-at-the-gate method is one that I object to on principle, and it is one that I have never been obliged to employ.'

They were speaking all the time in the

language of the harsh gutturals, and those who were in their vicinity looked at them in some perplexity, for it is a tongue unlike any that is heard in the Revolutionary Belt.

Closer and closer they grew to the inflexible inquisitor at the end of the police line. Ahead of them was a young man who turned from time to time as if seeking a friend behind. His was a face that fascinated the shorter of the two men, ever a student of faces. It was a face of deadly pallor, that the dark close-cropped hair and the thick black eyebrows accentuated. Aesthetic in outline, refined in contour, it was the face of a visionary, and in the restless, troubled eyes there lay a hint of the fanatic. He reached the barrier and a dozen eager men stepped forward for the honour of sponsorship. Then he passed and Manfred stepped calmly forward.

'Heinrich Rossenburg of Raz,' he mentioned the name of an obscure Transylvanian village.

'Who identifies this man?' asked Falmouth monotonously. Manfred held his breath and stood ready to spring.

'I do.'

It was the *spiritue* who had gone before him; the dreamer with the face of a priest.

'Pass.'

Manfred, calm and smiling, sauntered through the police with a familiar nod to his saviour. Then he heard the challenge that met his companion.

'Rolf Woolfund,' he heard Poiccart's clear, untroubled voice.

'Who identifies this man?'

Again he waited tensely.

'I do,' said the young man's voice again.

Then Poiccart joined him, and they waited a little.

Out of the corner of his eye Manfred saw the man who had vouched for him saunter toward them. He came abreast, then:

'If you would care to meet me at Reggiori's at King's Cross I shall be there in an hour,' he said, and Manfred noticed without emotion that this young man also spoke in Arabic.

They passed through the crowd that had gathered about the hall — for the news of the police raid had spread like wildfire through the East End — and gained Aldgate Station before they spoke.

'This is a curious beginning to our enterprise,' said Manfred. He seemed neither pleased nor sorry. 'I have always thought that Arabic was the safest language in the world in which to talk secrets — one learns wisdom with the years,' he added philosophically.

Poiccart examined his well-manicured

finger-nails as though the problem centred there. 'There is no precedent,' he said, speaking to himself.

'And he may be an embarrassment,' added George; then, 'let us wait and see what the hour brings.'

★   ★   ★

The hour brought the man who had befriended them so strangely. It brought also a little in advance of him a fourth man who limped slightly but greeted the two with a rueful smile. 'Hurt?' asked Manfred.

'Nothing worth speaking about,' said the other carelessly, 'and now what is the meaning of your mysterious telephone message?'

Briefly Manfred sketched the events of the night, and the other listened gravely.

'It's a curious situation,' he began, when a warning glance from Poiccart arrested him. The subject of their conversation had arrived.

He sat down at the table, and dismissed the fluttering waiter that hung about him.

The four sat in silence for a while and the newcomer was the first to speak.

'I call myself Bernard Courtlander,' he said simply, 'and you are the organization known as the Four Just Men.'

They did not reply.

'I saw you shoot,' he went on evenly, 'because I had been watching you from the moment when you entered the hall, and when the police adopted the method of identification, I resolved to risk my life and speak for you.'

'Meaning,' interposed Poiccart calmly, 'you resolved to risk — our killing you?'

'Exactly,' said the young man, nodding, 'a purely outside view would be that such a course would be a fiendish act of ingratitude, but I have a closer perception of principles, and I recognize that such a sequel to my interference is perfectly logical.' He singled out Manfred leaning back on the red plush cushions. 'You have so often shown that human life is the least considerable factor in your plan, and have given such evidence of your singleness of purpose, that I am fully satisfied that if my life — or the life of any one of you — stood before the fulfilment of your objects, that life would go — so!' He snapped his fingers.

'Well?' said Manfred.

'I know of your exploits,' the strange young man went on, 'as who does not?'

He took from his pocket a leather case, and from that he extracted a newspaper cutting. Neither of the three men evinced the slightest interest in the paper he unfolded on the white cloth. Their eyes were on his face.

'Here is a list of people slain — for justice's sake,' Courtlander said, smoothing the creases from a cutting from the *Megaphone*, 'men whom the law of the land passed by, sweaters and debauchers, robbers of public funds, corrupters of youth — men who bought 'justice' as you and I buy bread.' He folded the paper again. 'I have prayed God that I might one day meet you.'

'Well?' It was Manfred's voice again.

'I want to be with you, to be one of you, to share your campaign and . . . and — ' he hesitated, then added soberly, 'if need be, the death that awaits you.'

Manfred nodded slowly, then looked toward the man with the limp.

'What do you say, Gonsalez?' he asked.

This Leon Gonsalez was a famous reader of faces — that much the young man knew — and he turned for the test and met the other's appraising eyes.

'Enthusiast, dreamer, and intellectual, of course,' said Gonsalez slowly; 'there is reliability which is good, and balance which is better — but — '

'But — ?' asked Courtlander steadily.

'There is passion, which is bad,' was the verdict.

'It is a matter of training,' answered the other quietly. 'My lot has been thrown with people who think in a frenzy and act in madness; it is the fault of all the organizations that seek to right wrong by indiscriminate crime, whose sense are senses, who have debased sentiment to sentimentality, and who muddle kings with kingship.'

'You are of the Red Hundred?' asked Manfred.

'Yes,' said the other, 'because the Red Hundred carries me a little way along the road I wish to travel.'

'In the direction?'

'Who knows?' replied the other. 'There are no straight roads, and you cannot judge where lies your destination by the direction the first line of path takes.'

'I do not tell you how great a risk you take upon yourself,' said Manfred, 'nor do I labour the extent of the responsibility you ask to undertake. You are a wealthy man?'

'Yes,' said Courtlander, 'as wealth goes; I have large estates in Hungary.'

'I do not ask that question aimlessly, yet it would make no difference if you were poor,' said Manfred. 'Are you prepared to sell your estates — Buda-Gratz I believe they are called — Highness?'

For the first time the young man smiled.

31

'I did not doubt but that you knew me,' he said; 'as to my estates I will sell them without hesitation.'

'And place the money at my disposal?'

'Yes,' he replied, instantly. 'Without reservation?'

'Without reservation.'

'And,' said Manfred, slowly, 'if we felt disposed to employ this money for what might seem our own personal benefit, would you take exception?'

'None,' said the young man, calmly.

'And as a proof?' demanded Poiccart, leaning a little forward.

'The word of a Hap — '

'Enough,' said Manfred; 'we do not want your money — yet money is the supreme test.' He pondered awhile before he spoke again.

'There is the Woman of Gratz,' he said abruptly; 'at the worst she must be killed.'

'It is a pity,' said Courtlander, a little sadly. He had answered the final test did he but know it. A too willing compliance, an overeagerness to agree with the supreme sentence of the Four, any one thing that might have betrayed the lack of that exact balance of mind, which their word demanded, would have irretrievably condemned him.

'Let us drink an arrogant toast,' said

Manfred, beckoning a waiter. The wine was opened and the glasses filled, and Manfred muttered the toast.

'The Four who were three, to the Fourth who died and the Fourth who is born.'

★ ★ ★

Once upon a time there was a fourth who fell riddled with bullets in a Bordeaux cafe, and him they pledged. In Middlesex Street, in the almost emptied hall, Falmouth stood at bay before an army of reporters.

'Were they the Four Just Men, Mr. Falmouth?'

'Did you see them?'

'Have you any clue?'

Every second brought a fresh batch of newspaper men, taxi after taxi came into the dingy street, and the string of vehicles lined up outside the hall was suggestive of a fashionable gathering. The Telephone Tragedy was still fresh in the public mind, and it needed no more than the utterance of the magical words 'Four Just Men' to fan the spark of interest to flame again. The delegates of the Red Hundred formed a privileged throng in the little wilderness of a forecourt, and through these the journalists circulated industriously.

Smith of the *Megaphone* and his youthful assistant, Maynard, slipped through the crowd and found their taxi.

Smith shouted a direction to the driver and sank back in the seat with a whistle of weariness.

'Did you hear those chaps talking about police protection?' he asked; 'all the blessed anarchists from all over the world — and talking like a mothers' meeting! To hear 'em you would think they were the most respectable members of society that the world had ever seen. Our civilization is a wonderful thing,' he added, cryptically.

'One man,' said Maynard, 'asked me in very bad French if the conduct of the Four Just Men was actionable!'

At that moment, another question was being put to Falmouth by a leader of the Red Hundred, and Falmouth, a little ruffled in his temper, replied with all the urbanity that he could summon.

'You may have your meetings,' he said with some asperity, 'so long as you do not utter anything calculated to bring about a breach of the peace, you may talk sedition and anarchy till you're blue in the face. Your English friends will tell you how far you can go — and I might say you can go pretty far — you can advocate the assassination of kings, so long as you don't specify which king; you can plot against governments and denounce armies and grand dukes; in fact, you can do as you please — because that's the law.'

'What is — a breach of the peace?' asked his interrogator, repeating the words with difficulty.

Another detective explained.

★ ★ ★

Francois and one Rudulph Starque escorted the Woman of Gratz to her Bloomsbury lodgings that night, and they discussed the detective's answer.

This Starque was a big man, strongly built, with a fleshy face and little pouches under his eyes. He was reputed to be well off, and to have a way with women.

'So it would appear,' he said, 'that we may say 'Let the kings be slain,' but not 'Let the king be slain;' also that we may preach the downfall of governments, but if we say 'Let us go into this café' — how do you call it? — 'public-house, and be rude to the *proprietaire*' we commit a — er — breach of the peace — *ne c'est pas?*

'It is so,' said Francois, 'that is the English way.'

'It is a mad way,' said the other.

They reached the door of the girl's pension. She had been very quiet during the walk, answering questions that were put to her in monosyllables. She had ample food for thought in the events of the night.

Francois bade her a curt goodnight and walked a little distance. It had come to be regarded as Starque's privilege to stand nearest the girl. Now he took her slim hands in his and looked down at her. Some one has said the East begins at Bukarest, but there is a touch of the Eastern in every Hungarian, and there is a crudeness in their whole attitude to womankind that shocks the more tender susceptibilities of the Western.

'Goodnight, little Maria,' he said in a low voice. 'Some day you will be kinder, and you will not leave me at the door.'

She looked at him steadfastly. 'That will never be,' she replied, without a tremor.

3

Jessen, Alias Long

The front page of every big London daily was again black with the story of the Four Just Men.

'What I should like,' said the editor of the *Megaphone*, wistfully, 'is a sort of official propaganda from the Four — a sort of inspired manifesto that we could spread into six columns.'

Charles Garret, the *Megaphone's* 'star' reporter, with his hat on the back of his head, and an apparently inattentive eye fixed on the electrolier, sniffed. The editor looked at him reflectively.

'A smart man might get into touch with them.'

Charles said, 'Yes,' but without enthusiasm.

'If it wasn't that I knew you,' mused the editor, 'I should say you were afraid.'

'I am,' said Charles shamelessly.

'I don't want to put a younger reporter on this job,' said the editor sadly, 'it would look bad for you; but I'm afraid I must.'

'Do,' said Charles with animation, 'do, and

37

put me down ten shillings toward the wreath.'

He left the office a few minutes later with the ghost of a smile at the corners of his mouth, and one fixed determination in the deepest and most secret recesses of his heart. It was rather like Charles that, having by an uncompromising firmness established his right to refuse work of a dangerous character, he should of his own will undertake the task against which he had officially set his face. Perhaps his chief knew him as well as he knew himself, for as Charles, with a last defiant snort, stalked from the office, the smile that came to his lips was reflected on the editor's face.

Walking through the echoing corridors of Megaphone House, Charles whistled that popular and satirical song, the chorus of which runs —

By kind permission of the Megaphone,
By kind permission of the Megaphone.
Summer comes when Spring has gone,
And the world goes spinning on,
By permission of the Daily Megaphone.

Presently, he found himself in Fleet Street, and, standing at the edge of the curb, he answered a taxi-driver's expectant look with a nod.

'Where to, sir?' asked the driver.

'37 Presley Street, Walworth — round by the Blue Bob and the second turning to the left.'

Crossing Waterloo Bridge it occurred to him that the taxi might attract attention, so half-way down the Waterloo Road he gave another order, and, dismissing the vehicle, he walked the remainder of the way.

Charles knocked at 37 Presley Street, and after a little wait a firm step echoed in the passage, and the door was half opened. The passage was dark, but he could see dimly the thick-set figure of the man who stood waiting silently.

'Is that Mr. Long?' he asked.

'Yes,' said the man curtly.

Charles laughed, and the man seemed to recognize the voice and opened the door a little wider.

'Not Mr. Garrett?' he asked in surprise.

'That's me,' said Charles, and walked into the house.

His host stopped to fasten the door, and Charles heard the snap of the well-oiled lock and the scraping of a chain. Then with an apology the man pushed past him and, opening the door, ushered him into a well-lighted room, motioned Charles to a deep-seated chair, seated himself near a small table, turned down the page of the book from which he had evidently been reading, and looked inquiringly at his visitor.

'I've come to consult you,' said Charles.

A lesser man than Mr. Long might have been grossly flippant, but this young man — he was thirty-five, but looked older — did not descend to such a level.

'I wanted to consult you,' he said in reply.

His language was the language of a man who addresses an equal, but there was something in his manner which suggested deference.

'You spoke to me about Milton,' he went on, 'but I find I can't read him. I think it is because he is not sufficiently material.' He paused a little. 'The only poetry I can read is the poetry of the Bible, and that is because materialism and mysticism are so ingeniously blended — '

He may have seen the shadow on the journalist's face, but he stopped abruptly.

'I can talk about books another time,' he said. Charles did not make the conventional disclaimer, but accepted the other's interpretation of the urgency of his business.

'You know everybody,' said Charles, 'all the queer fish in the basket, and a proportion of them get to know you — in time.' The other nodded gravely.

'When other sources of information fail,' continued the journalist, 'I have never hesitated to come to you — Jessen.'

It may be observed that 'Mr. Long' at the threshold of the house became 'Mr. Jessen' in the intimacy of the inner room.

'I owe more to you than ever you can owe to me,' he said earnestly; 'you put me on the track,' he waved his hand round the room as though the refinement of the room was the symbol of that track of which he spoke. 'You remember that morning? — if you have forgotten, I haven't — when I told you that to forget — I must drink? And you said — '

'I haven't forgotten, Jessen,' said the correspondent quietly; 'and the fact that you have accomplished all that you have is a proof that there's good stuff in you.'

The other accepted the praise without comment.

'Now,' Charles went on, 'I want to tell you what I started out to tell: I'm following a big story. It's the Four Just Men story; you know all about it? I see that you do; well, I've got to get into touch with them somehow. I do not for one moment imagine that you can help me, nor do I expect that these chaps have any accomplices amongst the people you know.'

'They have not,' said Jessen; 'I haven't thought it worth while inquiring. Would you like to go to the Guild?'

Charles pursed his lips in thought.

'Yes,' he said slowly, 'that's an idea; yes, when?'

'Tonight — if you wish.'

'Tonight let it be,' said Charles.

His host rose and left the room.

He reappeared presently, wearing a dark overcoat and about his throat a black silk muffler that emphasized the pallor of his strong square face.

'Wait a moment,' he said, and unlocked a drawer, from which he took a revolver.

He turned the magazine carefully, and Charles smiled.

'Will that be necessary?' he asked.

Jessen shook his head.

'No,' he said with a little embarrassment, 'but — I have given up all my follies and fancies, but this one sticks.'

'The fear of discovery?'

Jessen nodded.

'It's the only folly left — this fear. It's the fly in the ointment.'

He led the way through the narrow passage, first having extinguished the lamp.

They stood together in the dark street, whilst Jessen made sure the fastening of the house.

'Now,' he said, and in a few minutes they

found themselves amidst the raucous confusion of a Walworth Road market-night.

They walked on in silence, then turning into East Street, they threaded a way between loitering shoppers, dodged between stalls overhung by flaring naphtha lamps, and turned sharply into a narrow street.

Both men seemed sure of their ground, for they walked quickly and unhesitatingly, and striking off through a tiny court that connected one malodorous thoroughfare with the other, they stopped simultaneously before the door of what appeared to be a disused factory.

A peaky-faced youth who sat by the door and acted as doorkeeper thrust his hand forward as they entered, but recognizing them drew back without a word.

They ascended the flight of ill-lighted stairs that confronted them, and pushing open a door at the head of the stairs, Jessen ushered his friend into a large hall.

It was a curious scene that met the journalist's eye. Well acquainted with 'the Guild' as he was, and with its extraordinary composition, he had never yet put his foot inside its portals. Basing his conception upon his knowledge of working-men's clubs and philanthropic institutions for the regeneration of degraded youth, he missed the inevitable billiard-table; he missed, too, the table strewn with month-old literature, but most of all he missed the smell of free coffee.

The floor was covered with sawdust, and about the fire that crackled and blazed at one end of the room there was a semicircle of chairs occupied by men of varying ages. Old-looking young men and young-looking old men, men in rags, men well dressed, men flashily attired in loud clothing and resplendent with shoddy jewellery. And they were drinking.

Two youths at one end of the crescent shared a quart pewter pot; the flashy man whose voice dominated the conversation held a glass of whisky in one be-ringed hand, and the white-haired man with the scarred face who sat with bowed head listening had a spirit glass half filled with some colourless fluid.

Nobody rose to greet the newcomers.

The flashy man nodded genially, and one of the circle pushed his chair back to give place to Jessen.

'I was just a-saying — ' said the flashy man, then looked at Charles.

'All right,' signalled Jessen.

'I was just a-sayin' to these lads,' continued the flashy one, 'that takin' one thing with the other, there's worse places than stir.'

Jessen made no reply to this piece of dogmatism, and he of the rings went on.

'An' what's the good of a man tryin' to go straight. The police will pull you all the same: not reportin' change of address, loitering with intent; it don't matter what you do if you've been in trouble once, you're sure to get in again.'

There was a murmur of assent.

'Look at me,' said the speaker with pride. 'I've never tried to go straight — been in twice an' it took six policemen to take me last time, and they had to use the stick.'

Jessen looked at him with mild curiosity.

'What does that prove, except that the policemen were pretty soft?'

'Not a bit!' The man stood up.

Under the veneer of tawdry foppery, Charles detected the animal strength of the criminal.

'Why, when I'm fit, as I am now,' the man went on, 'there ain't two policemen, nor four neither, that could handle me.'

Jessen's hand shot out and caught him by the forearm.

'Get away,' he suggested, and the man swung round like lightning, but Jessen had his other arm in a grip of iron. 'Get away,' he said again; but the man was helpless, and knew it, and after a pause Jessen released his hold.

'How was that?' he asked.

The amused smiles of the men did not embarrass the prisoner.

'The guv'nor's different,' he explained easily; 'he's got a knack of his own that the police haven't got.'

Jessen drew up a chair, and whatever there was in the action that had significance, it was sufficient to procure an immediate silence.

He looked round the attentive faces that were turned toward him. Charles, an interested spectator, saw the eager faces that bent in his friend's direction, and marvelled not a little at the reproductive qualities of the seed he had sown.

Jessen began to speak slowly, and Charles saw that what he said was in the nature of an address. That these addresses of Jessen were nothing unusual, and that they were welcome, was evident from the attention with which they were received.

'What Falk has been telling you,' said Jessen, indicating the man with the rings, 'is true — so far as it goes. There are worse places than stir, and it's true that the police don't give an old lag a chance, but that's because a lag won't change his job. And a lag won't change his job, because he doesn't know any other trade where he gets money so quickly. Wally' — he jerked his head toward a

46

weedy-looking youth — 'Wally there got a stretch for what? For stuff that fetched thirty pounds from a fence. Twelve months' hard work for thirty pounds! It works out at about 10s, 6d. a week. And his lawyer and the mouthpiece cost him a fiver out of that. Old man Garth' — he pointed to the white-headed man with the gin — 'did a five stretch for less than that, and he's out on brief. His wage works out at about a shilling a week.'

He checked the impatient motion that Falk made.

'I know that Falk would say,' he went on smoothly, 'that what I'm saying is outside the bargain; when I fixed up the Guild, I gave my 'davy that there wouldn't be any parson talk or Come All-ye-Faithful singing. Everybody knows that being on the crook's a mug's game, and I don't want to rub it in. What I've always said and done is in the direction of making you fellows earn bigger money at your own trade.

'There's a man who writes about the army who's been trying to induce soldiers to learn trades, and he started right by making the Tommies dissatisfied with their own trade; and that is what I am trying to do. What did I do with young Isaacs? I didn't preach at him, and I didn't pray over him. Ike was one of the finest snide merchants in London. He used to turn out half-crowns made from pewter pots that defied detection. They rang true and they didn't bend. Ike got three years, and when he came out I found him a job. Did I try to make him a wood-chopper, or a Salvation Army plough-boy? No. He'd have been back on the crook in a week if I had. I got a firm of medal makers in Birmingham to take him, and when Ike found himself amongst plaster moulds and electric baths, and discovered he could work at his own trade honestly, he stuck to it.'

'We ain't snide merchants,' growled Falk discontentedly.

'It's the same with all branches,' Jessen went on, 'only you chaps don't know it. Take tale-pitching — '

It would not be fair to follow Jessen through the elaborate disquisition by which he proved to the satisfaction of his audience that the 'confidence' man was a born commercial traveller. Many of his arguments were as unsound as they could well be; he ignored first principles, and glossed over what seemed to such a clear-headed hearer as Charles to be insuperable obstacles in the scheme of regeneration. But his audience was convinced. The fringe of men round the fire was reinforced as he continued. Men came into the room singly, and in twos and threes, and added themselves to the group at the fire. The news had spread that Jessen was talking — they called him Mr. Long, by the way — and some of the newcomers arrived breathlessly, as though they had run in order that no part of the address should be missed.

That the advocate of discontent had succeeded in installing into the minds of his hearers that unrest and dissatisfaction which he held to be the basis of a new moral code, was certain. For every face bore the stamp of introspective doubt.

Interesting as it all was, Charles Garrett had not lost sight of the object of his visit, and he fidgeted a little as the speaker proceeded.

Immediately on entering the room he had grasped the exact relationship in which Jessen stood to his pupils. Jessen he knew could put no direct question as to their knowledge of the Four Just Men without raising a feeling of suspicion which would have been fatal to the success of the mission, and indeed would have imperilled the very existence of the Guild.

It was when Jessen had finished speaking, and had answered a dozen questions fired simultaneously from a dozen quarters, and had answered the questions that had arisen out of these queries, that an opening came from an unexpected quarter.

For, with the serious business of the meeting disposed of, the questions took the inevitable facetious turn.

'What trade would you give the Four Just Men?' asked Falk flippantly, and there was a little rumble of laughter.

The journalist's eyes met the reformer's for one second, and through the minds of both men flashed the answer. Jessen's mouth twitched a little, and his restless hands were even more agitated as he replied slowly:

'If anybody can tell me exactly what the Four Just Men — what their particular line of business is, I could reply to that.'

It was the old man sipping his gin in silence who spoke for the first time.

'D'ye remember Billy Marks?' he asked.

His voice was harsh, as is that of a man who uses his voice at rare intervals.

'Billy Marks is dead,' he continued, 'deader than a door-nail. He knew the Four Just Men; pinched the watch an' the notebook of one an' nearly pinched them.'

There was a man who sat next to Falk who had been regarding Charles with furtive attention.

Now he turned to Jessen and spoke to the point. 'Don't get any idea in your head that the likes of us will ever have anything to do with the Four,' he said. 'Why, Mr. Long,' he went on, 'the Four Just Men are as likely to come to you as to us; bein' as you are a government official, it's very likely indeed.'

Again Jessen and Charles exchanged a swift glance, and in the eyes of the journalist was a strange light.

Suppose they came to Jessen! It was not unlikely. Once before, in pursuing their vengeance in a South American State, they had come to such a man as Jessen. It was a thought, and one worth following.

Turning the possibilities over in his mind Charles stood deep in thought as Jessen, still speaking, was helped into his overcoat by one of the men.

Then as they left the hall together, passing the custodian of the place at the foot of the stairs, the journalist turned to his companion.

'Should they come to you — ?'

Jessen shook his head.

'That is unlikely,' he said; 'they hardly require outside help.'

They walked the rest of the way in silence.

Charles shook hands at the door of Jessen's house.

'If by any chance they should come — ' he said.

Jessen laughed.

'I will let you know,' he said a little ironically.

Then he entered his house, and Charles heard again the snap of the lock as the strange man closed the door behind him.

★　★　★

Within twenty-four hours the newspapers recorded the mysterious disappearance of a Mr. J. Long, of Presley Street. Such a disappearance would have been without interest, but for a note that was found on his table. It ran:

Mr. Long being necessary for our purpose, we have taken him.
The Four Just Men

That the affair had connection with the Four was sufficient to give it an extraordinary news value. That the press was confounded goes without saying. For Mr. Long was a fairly unimportant man with some self-education and a craze for reforming the criminal classes. But the Home Office, which knew Mr. Long as Mr. Jessen, was greatly perturbed, and the genius of Scotland Yard was employed to discover his whereabouts.

4

The Red Bean

The Inner Council sent out an urgent call to the men who administer the affairs of the Red Hundred.

Starque came, Francois, the Frenchman, came, Hollom, the Italian, Paul Mirtisky, George Grabe, the American, and Lauder Bartholomew, the ex-captain of Irregular Cavalry, came also. Bartholomew was the best dressed of the men who gathered about the green table in Greek Street, for he had held the King's commission, which is of itself a sartorial education. People who met him vaguely remembered his name and frowned. They had a dim idea that there was 'something against him,' but were not quite sure what it was. It had to do with the South African War and a surrender — not an ordinary surrender, but an arrangement with the enemy on a cash basis, and the transference of stores. There was a court martial, and a cashiering, and afterwards Bartholomew came to England and bombarded first the War Office and then the press with a sheaf of type-written grievances. Afterwards he went into the theatrical line of business and appeared in music-hall sketches as 'Captain Lauder Bartholomew — the Hero of Dopfontein.'

There were other chapters which made good reading, for he figured in a divorce case, ran a society newspaper, owned a few selling platers, and achieved the distinction of appearing in the Racing Calendar in a paragraph which solemnly and officially forbade his presence on Newmarket Heath.

That he should figure on the Inner Council of the Red Hundred is remarkable only in so far as it demonstrates how much out of touch with British sentiments and conditions is the average continental politician. For Bartholomew's secret application to be enrolled a member of the Red Hundred had been received with acclamation and his promotion to the Inner Council had been rapid. Was he not an English officer — an aristocrat? A member of the most exclusive circle of English society? Thus argued the Red Hundred, to whom a subaltern in a scallywag corps did not differ perceptibly from a Commander of the Household Cavalry.

Bartholomew lied his way to the circle, because he found, as he had all along suspected, that there was a strong business end to terrorism. There were grants for secret service work, and with his fertile imagination it was not difficult to find excuses and reasons for approaching the financial executive of the Red Hundred at frequent intervals. He claimed intimacy with royal personages. He not only stated as a fact that he was in their confidence, but he suggested family ties which reflected little credit upon his progenitors.

The Red Hundred was a paying speculation; membership of the Inner Council was handsomely profitable. He had drawn a bow at a venture when under distress — literally it was a distress warrant issued at the instance of an importunate landlord — he had indited a letter to a revolutionary offering to act as London agent for an organization which was then known as The Friends of the People, but which has since been absorbed into the body corporate of the Red Hundred. It is necessary to deal fully with the antecedents of this man because he played a part in the events that are chronicled in the Council of Justice that had effects further reaching than Bartholomew, the mercenary of anarchism, could in his wildest moments have imagined.

He was one of the seven that gathered in the dingy drawing-room of a Greek Street boarding-house, and it was worthy of note that five of his fellows greeted him with a deference amounting to humility. The exception was Starque, who, arriving late, found an admiring circle hanging upon the words of this young man with the shifty eyes, and he frowned his displeasure.

Bartholomew looked up as Starque entered and nodded carelessly.

Starque took his place at the head of the table, and motioned impatiently to the others to be seated. One, whose duty it was, rose from his chair and locked the door. The windows were shuttered, but he inspected the fastenings; then, taking from his pocket two packs of cards, he scattered them in a confused heap upon the table. Every man produced a handful of money and placed it before him.

Starque was an ingenious man and had learnt many things in Russia. Men who gather round a green baize-covered table with locked doors are apt to be dealt with summarily if no adequate excuse for their presence is evident, and it is more satisfactory to be fined a hundred roubles for gambling than to be dragged off at a moment's notice to an indefinite period of labour in the mines on suspicion of being concerned in a revolutionary plot.

Starque now initiated the business of the

evening. If the truth be told, there was little in the earlier proceedings that differed from the procedure of the typical committee.

There were monies to be voted. Bartholomew needed supplies for a trip to Paris, where, as the guest of an *illustrious personage*, he hoped to secure information of vital importance to the Hundred.

'This is the fourth vote in two months, comrade,' said Starque testily, 'last time it was for information from your Foreign Office, which proved to be inaccurate.'

Bartholomew shrugged his shoulders with an assumption of carelessness.

'If you doubt the wisdom of voting the money, let it pass,' he said; 'my men fly high — I am not bribing policemen or *sous-officiers* of diplomacy.'

'It is not a question of money,' said Starque sullenly, 'it is a question of results. Money we have in plenty, but the success of our glorious demonstration depends upon the reliability of our information.'

The vote was passed, and with its passing came a grim element into the council.

Starque leant forward and lowered his voice.

'There are matters that need your immediate attention,' he said. He took a paper from his pocket, and smoothed it open in front of him. 'We have been so long inactive that the tyrants to whom the name of Red Hundred is full of terror, have come to regard themselves as immune from danger. Yet,' his voice sank lower, 'yet we are on the eve of the greatest of our achievements, when the oppressors of the people shall be moved at one blow! And we will strike a blow at kingship as shall be remembered in the history of the world aye, when the victories of Caesar and Alexander are forgotten and when the scenes of our acts are overlaid with the dust and debris of a thousand years. But that great day is not yet — first we must remove the lesser men that the blow may fall surer; first the servant, then the master.' He stabbed the list before him with a thick forefinger. 'Fritz von Hedlitz,' he read, 'Chancellor to the Duchy of Hamburg-Altoona.' He looked round the board and smiled. 'A man of some initiative, comrades — he foiled our attempt on his master with some cunning — do I interpret your desire when I say — death?'

'Death!'

It was a low murmured chorus.

Bartholomew, renegade and adventurer, said it mechanically. It was nothing to him a brave gentleman should die for no other reason than that he had served his master faithfully.

'Marquis de Santo-Strato, private secretary to the Prince of the Escorial,' read Starque.

'Death!' Again the murmured sentence.

One by one, Starque read the names, stopping now and again to emphasize some enormity of the man under review.

'Here is Hendrik Houssmann,' he said, tapping the paper, 'of the Berlin Secret Police: an interfering man and a dangerous one. He has already secured the arrest and punishment of one of our comrades.'

'Death,' murmured the council mechanically.

The list took half an hour to dispose of.

'There is another matter,' said Starque.

The council moved uneasily, for that other matter was uppermost in every mind.

'By some means we have been betrayed,' the chairman went on, and his voice lacked that confidence which characterized his earlier speech; 'there is an organization — an organization of reaction — which has set itself to thwart us. That organization has discovered our identity.' He paused a little. 'This morning I received a letter which named me president of the Inner Council and threatened me.' Again he hesitated. 'It was signed 'The Four Just Men.''

His statement was received in dead silence — a silence that perplexed him, for his compensation for the shock he had received had been the anticipation of the sensation his announcement would make.

He was soon enlightened as to the cause of the silence.

'I also have received a letter,' said Francois quietly.

'And I.'

'And I.'

'And I.'

Only Bartholomew did not speak, and he felt the unspoken accusation of the others.

'I have received no letter,' he said with an easy laugh — 'only these.' He fumbled in his waistcoat pocket and produced two beans. There was nothing peculiar in these save one was a natural black and the other had been dyed red.

'What do they mean?' demanded Starque suspiciously.

'I have not the slightest idea,' said Bartholomew with a contemptuous smile; 'they came in a little box, such as jewellery is sent in, and were unaccompanied either by letter or anything of the kind. These mysterious messages do not greatly alarm me.'

'But what does it mean?' persisted Starque, and every neck was craned toward the seeds; 'they must have some significance — think.'

Bartholomew yawned.

'So far as I know, they are beyond explanation,' he said carelessly; 'neither red nor black beans have played any conspicuous part in my life, so far as I — '

He stopped short and they saw a wave of colour rush to his face, then die away, leaving it deadly pale.

'Well?' demanded Starque; there was a menace in the question.

'Let me see,' faltered Bartholomew, and he took up the red bean with a hand that shook. He turned it over and over in his hand, calling up his reserve of strength. He could not explain, that much he realized.

The explanation might have been possible had he realized earlier the purport of the message he had received, but now with six pairs of suspicious eyes turned upon him, and with his confusion duly noted his hesitation would tell against him. He had to invent a story that would pass muster.

'Years ago,' he began, holding his voice steady, 'I was a member of such an organization as this: and — and there was a traitor.' The story was plain to him now, and he recovered his balance. 'The traitor was discovered and we balloted for his life. There was an equal number for death and immunity, and I as president had to give the casting vote. A red bean was for life and a black for death — and I cast my vote for the man's death.'

He saw the impression his invention had created and elaborated the story. Starque, holding the red bean in his hand, examined it carefully.

'I have reason to think that by my action I made many enemies, one of whom probably sent this reminder.' He breathed an inward sigh of relief as he saw the clouds of doubt lifting from the faces about him. Then —

'And the £1,000?' asked Starque quietly.

Nobody saw Bartholomew bite his lip, because his hand was caressing his soft black moustache. What they all observed was the well simulated surprise expressed in the lift of his eyebrows.

'The thousand pounds?' he said puzzled, then he laughed. 'Oh, I see you, too, have heard the story — we found the traitor had accepted that sum to betray us — and this we confiscated for the benefit of the Society — and rightly so,' he added, indignantly.

The murmur of approbation relieved him of any fear as to the result of his explanation. Even Starque smiled.

'I did not know the story,' he said, 'but I did see the '£1,000' which had been scratched on the side of the red bean; but this brings us no nearer to the solution of the mystery. Who has betrayed us to the Four Just Men?'

There came, as he spoke, a gentle tapping on the door of the room. Francois, who sat at the president's right hand, rose stealthily and tiptoed to the door.

'Who is there?' he asked in a low voice.

Somebody spoke in German, and the voice carried so that every man knew the speaker.

'The Woman of Gratz,' said Bartholomew, and in his eagerness he rose to his feet.

If one sought for the cause of friction between Starque and the ex-captain of Irregular Cavalry, here was the end of the search. The flame that came to the eyes of these two men as she entered the room told the story.

Starque, heavily made, animal man to his fingertips, rose to greet her, his face aglow.

'Madonna,' he murmured, and kissed her hand.

She was dressed well enough, with a rich sable coat that fitted tightly to her sinuous figure, and a fur toque upon her beautiful head.

She held a gloved hand toward Bartholomew and smiled.

Bartholomew, like his rival, had a way with women; but it was a gentle way, over laden with Western conventions and hedged about with set proprieties. That he was a contempt-ible villain according to our conceptions is true, but he had received a rudimentary training in the world of gentlemen. He had moved amongst men who took their hats off to their women kind, and who controlled their actions by a nebulous code. Yet he behaved with greater extravagance than did Starque, for he held her hand in his, looking into her eyes, whilst Starque fidgeted impatiently.

'Comrade,' at last he said testily, 'we will postpone our talk with our little Maria. It would be bad for her to think that she is holding us from our work — and there are the Four — '

He saw her shiver.

'The Four?' she repeated. 'Then they have written to you, also?'

Starque brought his fist with a crash down on the table.

'You — you! They have dared threaten you? By Heaven — '

'Yes,' she went on, and it seemed that her rich sweet voice grew a little husky; 'they have threatened — me.'

She loosened the furs at her throat as though the room had suddenly become hot and the atmosphere unbreathable.

The torrent of words that came tumbling to the lips of Starque was arrested by the look in her face.

'It isn't death that I fear,' she went on slowly; 'indeed, I scarcely know what I fear.'

Bartholomew, superficial and untouched by the tragic mystery of her voice, broke in upon their silence. For silenced they were by the girl's distress.

'With such men as we about, why need you notice the theatrical play of these Four Just Men?' he asked, with a laugh; then he remembered the two little beans and became suddenly silent with the rest.

So complete and inexplicable was the chill that had come to them with the pronouncement of the name of their enemy, and so absolutely did the spectacle of the Woman of Gratz on the verge of tears move them, that they heard then what none had heard before-the ticking of the clock.

It was the habit of many years that carried Bartholomew's hand to his pocket, mechanically he drew out his watch, and automatically he cast his eyes about the room for the clock wherewith to check the time.

It was one of those incongruous pieces of commonplace that intrude upon tragedy, but it loosened the tongues of the council, and they all spoke together.

It was Starque who gathered the girl's trembling hands between his plump palms.

'Maria, Maria,' he chided softly, 'this is folly. What! the Woman of Gratz who defied all Russia — who stood before Mirtowsky and bade him defiance — what is it?'

The last words were sharp and angry and were directed to Bartholomew.

For the second time that night the Englishman's face was white, and he stood clutching the edge of the table with staring eyes and with his lower jaw drooping.

'God, man!' cried Starque, seizing him by the arm, 'what is it — speak — you are frightening her!'

'The clock!' gasped Bartholomew in a hollow voice, 'where — where is the clock?'

His staring eyes wandered helplessly from side to side. 'Listen,' he whispered, and they held their breath. Very plainly indeed did they hear the 'tick — tick — tick.'

'It is under the table,' muttered Francois.

Starque seized the cloth and lifted it. Underneath, in the shadow, he saw the black box and heard the ominous whir of clockwork.

'Out!' he roared and sprang to the door. It was locked and from the outside.

Again and again he flung his huge bulk against the door, but the men who pressed round him, whimpering and slobbering in their pitiable fright, crowded about him and gave him no room.

With his strong arms he threw them aside left and right; then leapt at the door, bringing all his weight and strength to bear, and the door crashed open.

Alone of the party the Woman of Gratz preserved her calm. She stood by the table, her foot almost touching the accursed machine, and she felt the faint vibrations of its working. Then Starque caught her up in his arms and through the narrow passage he half led, half carried her, till they reached the street in safety.

The passing pedestrians saw the dishevelled group, and, scenting trouble, gathered about them.

'What was it? What was it?' whispered Francois, but Starque pushed him aside with a snarl.

A taxi was passing and he called it, and lifting the girl inside, he shouted directions and sprang in after her.

As the taxi whirled away, the bewildered Council looked from one to the other.

They had left the door of the house wide open and in the hall a flickering gas-jet gyrated wildly.

'Get away from here,' said Bartholomew

beneath his breath.

'But the papers — the records,' said the other wringing his hands.

Bartholomew thought quickly.

The records were such as could not be left lying about with impunity. For all he knew these madmen had implicated him in their infernal writings. He was not without courage, but it needed all he possessed to re-enter the room where a little machine in a black box ticked mysteriously.

'Where are they?' he demanded.

'On the table,' almost whispered the other. '*Mon Dieux!* what disaster!'

The Englishman made up his mind.

He sprang up the three steps into the hall. Two paces brought him to the door, another stride to the table. He heard the 'tick' of the machine, he gave one glance to the table and another to the floor, and was out again in the street before he had taken two long breaths.

Francois stood waiting, the rest of the men had disappeared.

'The papers! the papers!' cried the Frenchman.

'Gone!' replied Bartholomew between his teeth.

★   ★   ★

Less than a hundred yards away another conference was being held.

'Manfred,' said Poiccart suddenly — there had been a lull in the talk — 'shall we need our friend?' Manfred smiled. 'Meaning the admirable Mr. Jessen?'

Poiccart nodded.

'I think so,' said Manfred quietly; 'I am not so sure that the cheap alarm-clock we put in the biscuit box will be a sufficient warning to the Inner Council — here is Leon.'

Gonsalez walked into the room and removed his overcoat deliberately.

Then they saw that the sleeve of his dress coat was torn, and Manfred remarked the stained handkerchief that was lightly bound round one hand.

'Glass,' explained Gonsalez laconically. 'I had to scale a wall.'

'Well?' asked Manfred.

'Very well,' replied the other; 'they bolted like sheep, and I had nothing to do but to walk in and carry away the extremely interesting record of sentences they have passed.'

'What of Bartholomew?' Gonsalez was mildly amused. 'He was less panicky than the rest — he came back to look for the papers.'

'Will he — ?'

'I think so,' said Leon. 'I noticed he left the black bean behind him in his flight — so I presume we shall see the red.'

'It will simplify matters,' said Manfred gravely.

5

The Council of Justice

Lauder Bartholomew knew a man who was farming in Uganda. It was not remarkable that he should suddenly remember his friend's existence and call to mind a three years' old invitation to spend a winter in that part of Africa. Bartholomew had a club. It was euphemistically styled in all the best directories as 'Social, Literary and Dramatic', but knowing men about town called it by a shorter title. To them it was a 'night club'. Poorly as were the literary members catered for, there were certain weeklies, *The Times*, and a collection of complimentary timetables to be obtained for the asking, and Bartholomew sought and found particulars of sailings. He might leave London on the next morning and overtake (*via* Brindisi and Suez) the German boat that would land him in Uganda in a couple of weeks.

On the whole he thought this course would be wise.

To tell the truth, the Red Hundred was becoming too much of a serious business; he had a feeling that he was suspect, and was more certain that the end of his unlimited financing was in sight. That much he had long since recognized, and had made his plans accordingly. As to the Four Just Men, they would come in with Menshikoff; it would mean only a duplication of treachery. Turning the pages of a *Bradshaw*, he mentally reviewed his position. He had in hand some seven hundred pounds, and his liabilities were of no account because the necessity for discharging them never occurred to him. Seven hundred pounds — and the red bean, and Menshikoff.

'If they mean business,' he said to himself, 'I can count on three thousand.'

The obvious difficulty was to get into touch with the Four. Time was everything and one could not put an advertisement in the paper: *If the Four Just Men will communicate with L — B — they will hear of something to their advantage.*

Nor was it expedient to make in the agony columns of the London press even the most guarded reference to Red Beans after what had occurred at the Council Meeting. The matter of the Embassy was simple. Under his breath he cursed the Four Just Men for their unbusinesslike communication. If only they had mentioned or hinted at some rendezvous the thing might have been arranged.

A man in evening dress asked him if he had finished with the *Bradshaw*. He resigned it ungraciously, and calling a club waiter, ordered a whisky and soda and flung himself into a chair to think out a solution.

The man returned the Bradshaw with a polite apology.

'So sorry to have interrupted, but I've been called abroad at a moment's notice,' he said.

Bartholomew looked up resentfully. This young man's face seemed familiar.

'Haven't I met you somewhere?' he asked.

The stranger shrugged his shoulders.

'One is always meeting and forgetting,' he smiled. 'I thought I knew you, but I cannot quite place you.'

Not only the face but the voice was strangely familiar.

'Not English,' was Bartholomew's mental analysis, 'possibly French, more likely Slav — who the dickens can it be?'

In a way he was glad of the diversion, and found himself engaged in a pleasant discussion on fly fishing.

As the hands of the clock pointed to midnight, the stranger yawned and got up from his chair.

'Going west?' he asked pleasantly.

Bartholomew had no definite plans for

spending the next hour, so he assented and the two men left the club together. They strolled across Piccadilly Circus and into Piccadilly, chatting pleasantly.

Through Half Moon Street into Berkeley Square, deserted and silent, the two men sauntered, then the stranger stopped.

'I'm afraid I've taken you out of your way,' he said.

'Not a bit,' replied Bartholomew, and was conventionally amiable.

Then they parted, and the ex-captain walked back by the way he had come, picking up again the threads of the problem that had filled his mind in the earlier part of the evening.

Halfway down Half Moon Street was a motor-car, and as he came abreast, a man who stood by the curb — and whom he had mistaken for a waiting chauffeur — barred his further progress.

'Captain Bartholomew?' he asked respectfully.

'That is my name,' said the other in surprise.

'My master wishes to know whether you have decided.'

'What — ?'

'If,' went on his imperturbable examiner, 'if you have decided on the red — here is the car, if you will be pleased to enter.'

'And if I have decided on the black?' he asked with a little hesitation.

'Under the circumstances,' said the man without emotion, 'my master is of opinion that for his greater safety, he must take steps to ensure your neutrality.'

There was no menace in the tone, but an icy matter-of-fact confidence that shocked this hardened adventurer.

In the dim light he saw something in the man's hand — a thin bright something that glittered.

'It shall be red!' he said hoarsely.

The man bowed and opened the door of the car.

Bartholomew had regained a little of his self-assurance by the time he stood before the men.

He was not unused to masked tribunals. There had been one such since his elevation to the Inner Council.

But these four men were in evening dress, and the stagey setting that had characterized the Red Hundred's Court of Justice was absent. There was no weird adjustment of lights, or rollings of bells, or partings of sombre draperies. None of the cheap trickery of the Inner Council.

The room was evidently a drawing-room,

very much like a hundred other drawing-rooms he had seen.

The four men who sat at equal distance before him were sufficiently ordinary in appearance save for their masks. He thought one of them wore a beard, but he was not sure. This man did most of the speaking.

'I understand,' he said smoothly, 'you have chosen the red.'

'You seem to know a great deal about my private affairs,' replied Bartholomew.

'You have chosen the red — again?' said the man.

'Why — again?' demanded the prisoner.

The masked man's eyes shone steadily through the holes in the mask. 'Years ago,' he said quietly, 'there was an officer who betrayed his country and his comrades.'

'That is an old lie.'

'He was in charge of a post at which was stored a great supply of foodstuffs and ammunition,' the mask went on. 'There was a commandant of the enemy who wanted those stores, but had not sufficient men to rush the garrison.'

'An old lie,' repeated Bartholomew sullenly.

'So the commandant hit upon the ingenious plan of offering a bribe. It was a risky thing, and in nine hundred and ninety-nine cases out of a thousand, it would have been a futile business. Indeed, I am sure that I am understating the proportion — but the wily old commandant knew his man.'

'There is no necessity to continue,' said Bartholomew.

'No correspondence passed,' Manfred went on; 'our officer was too cunning for that, but it was arranged that the officer's answer should be conveyed thus.'

He opened his hand and Bartholomew saw two beans, one red and the other black, reposing in the palm.

'The black was to be a refusal, the red an acceptance, the terms were to be scratched on the side of the red bean with a needle — and the sum agreed was £1,000.'

Bartholomew made no answer.

'Exactly that sum we offer you to place us from time to time in possession of such information as we require concerning the movements of the Red Hundred.'

'If I refuse?'

'You will not refuse,' replied the mask calmly; 'you need the money, and you have even now under consideration a plan for cutting yourself adrift from your friends.'

'You know so much — ' began the other with a shrug.

'I know a great deal. For instance, I know that you contemplate immediate flight — by the way, are you aware that the *Lucus Woerhmann* is in dock at Naples with a leaking boiler?'

Bartholomew started, as well he might, for nobody but himself knew that the *Lucus Woerhmann* was the ship he had hoped to overtake at Suez.

Manfred saw his bewilderment and smiled.

'I do not ask credit for supernatural powers,' he said; 'frankly, it was the merest guesswork, but you must abandon your trip. It is necessary for our greater success that you should remain.'

Bartholomew bit his lips. This scheme did not completely fall in with his plans. He affected a sudden geniality.

'Well, if I must, I must,' he said heartily, 'and since I agree, may I ask whom I have the honour of addressing, and further, since I am now your confidential agent, that I may see the faces of my employers?'

He recognized the contempt in Manfred's laugh.

'You need no introduction to us,' said Manfred coldly, 'and you will understand we do not intend taking you into our confidence. Our agreement is that we share your confidence, not that you shall share ours.'

'I must know something,' said Bartholomew doggedly. 'What am I to do? Where am I to report! How shall I be paid?'

'You will be paid when your work is completed.' Manfred reached out his hand toward a little table that stood within his reach.

Instantly the room was plunged into darkness.

The traitor sprang back, fearing he knew not what.

'Come — do not be afraid,' said a voice.

'What does this mean?' cried Bartholomew, and stepped forward.

He felt the floor beneath him yield and tried to spring backwards, but already he had lost his balance, and with a scream of terror he felt himself falling, falling . . .

★   ★   ★

'Here, wake up!'

Somebody was shaking his arm and he was conscious of an icy coldness and a gusty raw wind that buffeted his face.

He shivered and opened his eyes.

First of all he saw an iron camel with a load on its back; then he realized dimly that it was the ornamental support of a garden seat; then he saw a dull grey parapet of grimy stone. He was sitting on a seat on the Thames Embankment, and a policeman was shaking him, not ungently, to wakefulness.

'Come along, sir — this won't do, ye know.'

He staggered to his feet unsteadily. He was wearing a fur coat that was not his.

'How did I come here?' he asked in a dull voice.

The policeman laughed good humouredly.

'Ah, that's more than I can tell you — you weren't here ten minutes ago, that I'll swear.'

Bartholomew put his hand in his pocket and found some money.

'Call me a taxi,' he said shakily and one was found.

He left the policeman perfectly satisfied with the result of his morning's work and drove home to his lodgings. By what extraordinary means had he reached the Embankment? He remembered the Four, he remembered the suddenly darkened room, he remembered falling — Perhaps he lost consciousness, yet he could not have been injured by his fall. He had a faint recollection of somebody telling him to breathe and of inhaling a sweet sickly vapour — and that was all.

The coat was not his. He thrust his hands into both pockets and found a letter. Did he but know it was of the peculiar texture that had made the greenish-grey paper of the Four Just Men famous throughout Europe.

The letter was brief and to the point:

For faithful service, you will be rewarded; for treachery, there will be no net to break your fall.

He shivered again. Then his impotence, his helplessness, enraged him, and he swore softly and weakly. He was ignorant of the locality in which the interview had taken place. On his way thither he had tried in vain to follow the direction the shuttered motor-car had taken.

By what method the Four would convey their instructions he had no idea. He was quite satisfied that they would find a way.

He reached his flat with his head swimming from the effects of the drug they had given him, and flung himself, dressed as he was, upon his bed and slept. He slept well into the afternoon, then rose stiff and irritable. A bath and a change refreshed him, and he walked out to keep an appointment he had made.

On his way he remembered impatiently that there was a call to the Council at five o'clock. It reminded him of his old rehearsal days. Then he recollected that no place had been fixed for the council meeting. He would find the quiet Francois in Leicester Square, so he turned his steps in that direction.

Francois, patient, smiling, and as deferential as ever, awaited him.

'The council was held at two o'clock,' he said, 'and I am to tell you that we have decided on two projects.' He looked left and right, with elaborated caution. 'There is at Gravesend' — he pronounced it 'Gwayvse-end' — 'a battleship that has put in for stores. It is the *Grondovitch*. It will be fresh in your mind that the captain is the nobleman Svardo — we have no reason to love him.'

'And the second?' asked Bartholomew.

Again Francois went through the pantomime that had so annoyed his companion before.

'It is no less than the Bank,' he said triumphantly.

Bartholomew was aghast.

'The Bank — the Bank of England! Why, you're mad — you have taken leave of your senses!'

Francois shrugged his shoulders tolerantly.

'It is the order,' he said; then, abruptly, '*Au revoir*,' he said, and, with his extravagant little bow, was gone.

If Bartholomew's need for cutting himself adrift from the Red Hundred existed before, the necessity was multiplied now a thousand times. Any lingering doubt he might have had, any remote twinge of conscience at the part he was playing, these vanished.

He glanced at his watch, and hurried to his destination.

It was the Red Room of the Hotel Larboune that he sought.

He found a table and ordered a drink. The waiter was unusually talkative.

He stood by the solitary table at which Bartholomew sat, and chatted pleasantly and respectfully. This much the other patrons of the establishment noticed idly, and wondered whether it was racing or house property that the two had in common.

The waiter was talking.

' . . . I am inclined to disbelieve the story of the *Grondovitch*, but the Embassy and the commander shall know — when do you leave?'

'Just as soon as I can,' said Bartholomew.

The waiter nodded and flicked some cigarette ash from the table with his napkin.

'And the Woman of Gratz?' he asked.

Bartholomew made a gesture of doubt.

'Why not,' said the waiter, looking thoughtfully out of the window, 'why not take her with you?'

There had been the germ of such a thought in Bartholomew's mind, but he had never given form to it — even to himself.

'She is very beautiful, and, it occurred to

me, not altogether indifferent to your attractions — that kind of woman has a penchant for your type, and frankly we would gladly see her out of the way — or dead.'

M. Menshikoff was by no means vindictive, but there was obvious sincerity in his voice when he pronounced the last two words. M. Menshikoff had been right-hand man of the Grand Master of the Secret Police for too many years to feel any qualms at the project of removing an enemy to the system.

'I thought we had her once,' he said meditatively; 'they would have flogged her in the fortress of St Peter and Paul, but I stopped them. She was grateful I think, and almost human . . . but it passed off.'

Bartholomew paid for his drink, and ostentatiously tipped the obsequious man before him. He remembered as he did so that Menshikoff was reputedly a millionaire.

'Your change, *m'sieur*,' said Menshikoff gravely, and he handed back a few jingling coppers and two tightly folded banknotes for a hundred pounds. He was a believer in the principle of 'pay as you go'. Bartholomew pocketed the money carelessly.

'Good day,' he said loudly.

'*Au revoir, m'sieur, et bon voyage*,' said the waiter.

6

Princess Revolutionary

The Woman of Gratz was very human. But to Bartholomew she seemed a thing of ice, passionless, just a beautiful woman who sat stiffly in a straight-backed chair, regarding him with calm, questioning eyes. They were in her flat in Bloomsbury on the evening of the day following his interview with Menshikoff. Her coolness chilled him, and strangled the very passion of his speech, and what he said came haltingly, and sounded lame and unconvincing.

'But why?' that was all she asked. Thrice he had paused appealingly, hoping for encouragement, but her answer had been the same.

He spoke incoherently, wildly. The fear of the Four on the one hand and the dread of the Reds on the other, were getting on his nerves.

He saw a chance of escape from both, freedom from the four-walled control of these organizations, and before him the wide expanse of a trackless wilderness, where the vengeance of neither could follow.

Eden in sight — he pleaded for an Eve.

The very thought of the freedom ahead overcame the depression her coldness laid upon him.

'Maria — don't you see? You are wasting your life doing this man's work — this assassin's work. You were made for love and for me!' He caught her hand and she did not withdraw it, but the palm he pressed was unresponsive and the curious searching eyes did not leave his face.

'But why?' she asked again. 'And how? I do not love you, I shall never love any man — and there is the work for you and the work for me. There is the cause and your oath. Your comrades — '

He started up and flung away her hand. For a moment he stood over her, glowering down at her upturned face.

'Work! — Comrades!' he grated with a laugh. 'D'ye think I'm going to risk my precious neck any further?'

He did not hear the door open softly, nor the footfall of the two men who entered.

'Are you blind as well as mad?' he went on brutally. 'Don't you see that the thing is finished? The Four Just Men have us all in the hollow of their hands! They've got us like that!' He snapped his fingers contemptuously. 'They know everything — even to the attempt that is to be made on the Prince of the Escorials! Ha! that startles you — yet it is true, every word I say — they know.'

'If it is true,' she said slowly, 'there has been a traitor.'

He waved his hand carelessly, admitting and dismissing the possibility.

'There are traitors always — when the pay for treachery is good,' he said easily; 'but traitor or no traitor, London is too hot for you and me.'

'For you,' corrected the girl.

'And for you,' he said savagely; he snatched up her hand again. 'You've got to come — do you hear — you beautiful snow woman — you've got to come with me!'

He drew her to him, but a hand grasped his arm, and he turned to meet the face of Starque, livid and puckered, and creased with silent anger.

Starque was prepared for the knife or for the pistol, but not for the blow that caught him full in the face and sent him staggering back to the wall.

He recovered himself quickly, and motioned to Francois, who turned and locked the door.

'Stand away from that door!'

'Wait!'

Starque, breathing quickly, wiped the blood

from his face with the back of his hand.

'Wait,' he said in his guttural tone; 'before you go there is a matter to be settled.'

'At any time, in any place,' said the Englishman.

'It is not the blow,' breathed Starque, 'that is nothing; it is the matter of the Inner Council — traitor!'

He thrust out his chin as he hissed the last word.

Bartholomew had very little time to decide upon his course of action. He was unarmed; but he knew instinctively that there would be no shooting. It was the knife he had to fear and he grasped the back of a chair. If he could keep them at a distance he might reach the door and get safely away. He cursed his folly that he had delayed making the *coup* that would have so effectively laid Starque by the heels.

'You have betrayed us to the Four Just Men — but that we might never have known, for the Four have no servants to talk. But you sold us to the Embassy — and that was your undoing.' He had recovered his calm.

'We sent you a message telling you of our intention to destroy the Bank of England. The Bank was warned — by the Four. We told you of the attempt to be made on the *Grondovitch* — the captain was warned by the Embassy — you are doubly convicted. No such attempts were ever contemplated. They were invented for your particular benefit, and you fell into the trap.'

Bartholomew took a fresh grip of the chair. He realized vaguely that he was face to face with death, and for one second he was seized with a wild panic.

'Last night,' Starque went on deliberately, 'the Council met secretly, and your name was read from the list.' The Englishman's mouth went dry.

'And the Council said with one voice . . . ' Starque paused to look at the Woman of Gratz. Imperturbable she stood with folded hands, neither approving nor dissenting. Momentarily Bartholomew's eyes too sought her face — but he saw neither pity nor condemnation. It was the face of Fate, inexorable, unreasoning, inevitable.

'Death was the sentence,' said Starque in so soft a voice that the man facing him could scarcely hear him. 'Death . . . ' With a lightning motion he raised his hand and threw the knife . . .

'Damn you . . . ' whimpered the stricken man, and his helpless hands groped at his chest . . . then he slid to his knees and Francois struck precisely . . .

Again Starque looked at the woman.

'It is the law,' he stammered, but she made no reply.

Only her eyes sought the huddled figure on the floor and her lips twitched.

'We must get away from here,' whispered Starque.

He was shaking a little, for this was new work for him. The forces of jealousy and fear for his personal safety had caused him to take upon himself the office that on other occasions he left to lesser men.

'Who lives in the opposite flat?'

He had peeped through the door.

'A student — a chemist,' she replied in her calm, level tone.

Starque flushed, for her voice sounded almost strident coming after the whispered conference between his companion and himself.

'Softly, softly,' he urged.

He stepped gingerly back to where the body was lying, made a circuit about it, and pulled down the blind. He could not have explained the instinct that made him do this. Then he came back to the door and gently turned the handle, beckoning the others. It seemed to him that the handle turned itself, or that somebody on the other side was turning at the same time.

That this was so he discovered, for the door

suddenly jerked open, sending him staggering backward, and a man stood on the threshold.

With the drawn blind, the room was in semi-darkness, and the intruder, standing motionless in the doorway, could see nothing but the shadowy figures of the inmates.

As he waited he was joined by three others, and he spoke rapidly in a language that Starque, himself no mean linguist, could not understand. One of his companions opened the door of the student's room and brought out something that he handed to the watcher on the threshold.

Then the man entered the room alone and closed the door behind him, not quite close, for he had trailed what looked like a thick cord behind him and this prevented the shutting of the door.

Starque found his voice.

'What do you want?' he asked, quietly.

'I want Bartholomew, who came into this room half an hour ago,' replied the intruder.

'He has left,' said Starque, and in the darkness he felt at his feet for the dead man — he needed the knife.

'That is a lie,' said the stranger coolly; 'neither he nor you, Rudolph Starque, nor the Woman of Gratz, nor the murderer Francois has left.'

'*Monsieur* knows too much,' said Starque

91

evenly, and lurched forward, swinging his knife.

'Keep your distance,' warned the stranger, and at that moment Starque and the silent Francois sprang forward and struck . . .

The exquisite agony of the shock that met them paralysed them for the moment. The sprayed threads of the 'live' wire the man held before him like a shield jerked the knife from Starque's hands, and he heard Francois groan as he fell.

'You are foolish,' said the voice again, 'and you, *madame*, do not move, I beg — tell me what has become of Bartholomew.'

A silence, then:

'He is dead,' said the Woman of Gratz.

She heard the man move.

'He was a traitor — so we killed him,' she continued calmly enough. 'What will you do — you, who stand as a self-constituted judge?'

He made no reply, and she heard the soft rustle of his fingers on the wall.

'You are seeking the light — as we all seek it,' she said, unmoved, and she switched on the light.

He saw her standing near the body of the man she had lured to his death, scornful, defiant, and strangely aloof from the sordidness of the tragedy she had all but instigated.

She saw a tanned man of thirty-five, with deep, grave eyes, a broad forehead, and a trim, pointed beard. A man of inches, with strength in every line of his fine figure, and strength in every feature of his face.

She stared at him insolently, uncaring, but before the mastery of his eyes, she lowered her lids.

It seemed the other actors in the drama were so inconsiderate as to be unworthy of notice. The dead man in his grotesque posture, the unconscious murderer at his feet, and Starque, dazed and stunned, crouching by the wall.

'Here is the light you want,' she went on, 'not so easily do we of the Red Hundred illuminate the gloom of despair and oppression — '

'Spare me your speech-making,' said Manfred coldly, and the scorn in his voice struck her like the lash of a whip. For the first time the colour came to her face and her eyes lit with anger.

'You have bad counsellors,' Manfred went on, 'you, who talk of autocrats and corrupt kingship — what are you but a puppet living on flattery? It is your whim that you should be regarded as a conspirator — a Corday. And when you are acclaimed Princess Revolutionary, it is satisfactory to your vanity

— more satisfactory than your title to be hailed Princess Beautiful.'

He chose his words nicely.

'Yet men — such men as these,' he indicated Starque, 'think only of the Princess Beautiful — not the lady of the Inspiring Platitudes; not the frail, heroic Patriot of the Flaming Words, but the warm flesh and blood woman, lovable and adorable.'

He spoke in German, and there were finer shades of meaning in his speech than can be exactly or literally translated. He spoke of a purpose, evenly and without emotion. He intended to wound, and wound deeply, and he knew he had succeeded.

He saw the rapid rise and fall of her bosom as she strove to regain control of herself, and he saw, too, the blood on her lips where her sharp white teeth bit.

'I shall know you again,' she said with an intensity of passion that made her voice tremble. 'I shall look for you and find you, and be it the Princess Revolutionary or the Princess Beautiful who brings about your punishment, be sure I shall strike hard.'

He bowed.

'That is as it may be,' he said calmly; 'for the moment you are powerless, if I willed it you would be powerless forever — for the moment it is my wish that you should go.'

He stepped aside and opened the door.

The magnetism in his eyes drew her forward.

'There is your road,' he said when she hesitated. She was helpless; the humiliation was maddening.

'My friends — ' she began, as she hesitated on the threshold.

'Your friends will meet the fate that one day awaits you,' he said calmly.

White with passion, she turned on him.

'You! — threaten me! a brave man indeed to threaten a woman!'

She could have bitten her tongue at the slip she made. She as a woman had appealed to him as a man! This was the greatest humiliation of all.

There is your road,' he said again, courteously but uncompromisingly.

She was scarcely a foot from him, and she turned and faced him, her lips parted and the black devil of hate in her eyes.

'One day — one day,' she gasped, 'I will repay you!'

Then she turned quickly and disappeared through the door, and Manfred waited until her footsteps had died away before he stooped to the half-conscious Starque and jerked him to his feet.

7

The Government and Mr. Jessen

In recording the events that followed the reappearance of the Four Just Men, I have confined myself to those which I know to have been the direct outcome of the Red Hundred propaganda and the counter-activity of the Four Just Men.

Thus I make no reference to the explosion at Woolwich Arsenal, which was credited to the Red Hundred, knowing, as I do, that the calamity was due to the carelessness of a workman. Nor to the blowing up of the main in Oxford Street, which was a much more simple explanation than the fantastic theories of the *Megaphone* would have you imagine. This was not the first time that a fused wire and a leaking gas main brought about the upheaval of a public thoroughfare, and the elaborate plot with which organized anarchy was credited was without existence.

I think the most conscientiously accurate history of the Red Hundred movement is that set forth in the series of ten articles contributed to the *Morning Leader* by

Harold Ashton under the title of *Forty Days of Terrorism*, and, whilst I think the author frequently fails from lack of sympathy for the Four Just Men to thoroughly appreciate the single-mindedness of this extraordinary band of men, yet I shall always regard *Forty Days of Terrorism* as being the standard history of the movement, and its failure.

On one point in the history alone I find myself in opposition to Mr. Ashton, and that is the exact connection between the discovery of the Carlby Mansion Tragedy, and the extraordinary return of Mr. Jessen of 37 Presley Street.

It is perhaps indiscreet of me to refer at so early a stage to this return of Jessen's, because whilst taking exception to the theories put forward in *Forty Days of Terrorism*, I am not prepared to go into the evidence on which I base my theories.

The popular story is that one morning Mr. Jessen walked out of his house and demanded from the astonished milkman why he had omitted to leave his morning supply. Remembering that the disappearance of Long — perhaps it would be less confusing to call him the name by which he was known in Presley Street — had created an extraordinary sensation; that pictures of his house and the interior of his house had appeared in all

97

the newspapers; that the newspaper crime experts had published columns upon columns of speculative theories, and that 37 Presley Street, had for some weeks been the Mecca of the morbid minded, who, standing outside, stared the unpretentious façade out of countenance for hours on end; you may imagine that the milkman legend had the exact journalistic touch that would appeal to a public whose minds had been trained by generations of magazine-story writers to just such *denouement* as this.

The truth is that Mr. Long, upon coming to life, went immediately to the Home Office and told his story to the Under Secretary. He did not drive up in a taxi, nor was he lifted out in a state of exhaustion as one newspaper had erroneously had it, but he arrived on the top of a motor omnibus which passed the door, and was ushered into the *presence* almost at once. When Mr. Long had told his story he was taken to the Home Secretary himself, and the chief commissioner was sent for, and came hurriedly from Scotland Yard, accompanied by Superintendent Falmouth. All this is made clear in Mr. Ashton's book.

For some extraordinary reason, (I quote the same authority,) Long, or Jessen, seems by means of documents in his possession to have explained to the satisfaction of the Home Secretary and the Police Authorities his own position in the matter, and moreover to have inspired the right hon. gentleman with these mysterious documents, that Mr. Ridgeway, so far from accepting the resignation that Jessen placed in his hands, reinstated him in his position.

As to how two of these documents came to Jessen or to the Four Just Men, Mr. Ashton is very wisely silent, not attempting to solve a mystery which puzzled both the Quai d'Orsay and Petrograd.

For these two official forms, signed in the one case by the French President and in the other with the sprawling signature of Czar Nicholas, were supposed to be incorporated with other official memoranda in well-guarded national archives.

It was subsequent to Mr. Jessen's visit to the Home Office that the discovery of the Garlby Mansions Tragedy was made, and I cannot do better than quote *The Times*, since that journal, jealous of the appearance in its columns of any news of a sensational character, reduced the intelligence to its most constricted limits. Perhaps the *Megaphone* account might make better reading, but the space at my disposal will not allow of the inclusion in this book of the thirty-three columns of reading matter, headlines, portraits, and diagrammatic illustrations with which that enterprising journal served up particulars of the grisly horror to its readers. Thus, *The Times*:

Shortly after one o'clock yesterday afternoon and in consequence of information received, Superintendent Falmouth, of the Criminal Investigation Department, accompanied by Detective-Sergeants Boyle and Lawley, effected an entrance into No. 69, Carlby Mansions, occupied by the Countess Slienvitch, a young Russian lady of independent means. Lying on the floor were the bodies of three men who have since been identified as:
Lauder Bartholomew, aged 33, late of the Koondorp Mounted Rifles; Rudolph Starque, aged 40, believed to be an Austrian and a prominent revolutionary propagandist;
Henri Delaye Francois, aged 36, a Frenchman, also believed to have been engaged in propaganda work.
The cause of death in the case of Bartholomew seems to be evident, but with the other two men some doubt exists, and the police, who preserve an attitude of rigid reticence, will await the medical examination before making any statement. One

unusual feature of the case is understood to be contained in a letter found in the room accepting, on behalf of an organization known as the Four Just Men, full responsibility for the killing of the two foreigners, and another, writes a correspondent, is the extraordinary structural damage to the room itself. The tenant, the Countess Slienvitch, had not, up to a late hour last night, been traced.

★ ★ ★

Superintendent Falmouth, standing in the centre of the room, from which most traces of the tragedy had been removed, was mainly concerned with the 'structural damage' that *The Times* so lightly passed over.

At his feet yawned a great square hole, and beneath, in the empty flat below, was a heap of plaster and laths, and the debris of destruction.

'The curious thing is, and it shows how thorough these men are,' explained the superintendent to his companion, 'that the first thing we found when we got there was a twenty-pound note pinned to the wall with a brief note in pencil saying that this was to pay the owner of the property for the damage.'

It may be added that by the express desire

of the young man at his side he dispensed with all ceremony of speech.

Once or twice in speaking, he found himself on the verge of saying, 'Your Highness', but the young man was so kindly, and so quickly put the detective at his ease, that he overcame the feeling of annoyance that the arrival of the distinguished visitor with the letter from the commissioner had caused him, and became amiable.

'Of course, I have an interest in all this,' said the young man quietly; 'these people, for some reason, have decided I am not fit to encumber the earth — '

'What have you done to the Red Hundred, sir?'

The young man laughed.

'Nothing. On the contrary,' he added with a whimsical smile, 'I have helped them.'

The detective remembered that this hereditary Prince of the Escorial bore a reputation for eccentricity.

With a suddenness which was confusing, the Prince turned with a smile on his lips.

'You are thinking of my dreadful reputation?'

'No, no!' disclaimed the embarrassed Mr. Falmouth. 'I — '

'Oh, yes — I've done lots of things,' said the other with a little laugh; 'it's in the blood

— my illustrious cousin — '

'I assure your Highness,' said Falmouth impressively, 'my reflections were not — er — reflections on yourself — there is a story that you have dabbled in socialism — but that, of course — '

'Is perfectly true,' concluded the Prince calmly. He turned his attention to the hole in the floor.

'Have you any theory?' he asked.

The detective nodded.

It's more than a theory — it's knowledge — you see we've seen Jessen, and the threads of the story are all in hand.'

'What will you do?'

'Nothing,' said the detective stolidly; 'hush up the inquest until we can lay the Four Just Men by the heels.'

'And the manner of killing?'

'That must be kept quiet,' replied Falmouth emphatically.

This conversation may furnish a clue as to the unprecedented conduct of the police at the subsequent inquest.

★ ★ ★

In the little coroner's court there was accommodation for three pressmen and some fifty of the general public. Without desiring in any way to cast suspicion upon the cleanest police force in the world, I can only state that the jury were remarkably well disciplined, that the general public found the body of the court so densely packed with broad-shouldered men that they were unable to obtain admission. As to the press, the confidential circular had done its work, and the three shining lights of journalism that occupied the reporters' desk were careful to carry out instructions.

The proceedings lasted a very short time, a verdict, ' . . . some person or persons unknown,' was recorded, and another London mystery was added (I quote from the Evening News) to the already alarming and formidable list of unpunished crimes.

Charles Garrett was one of the three journalists admitted to the inquest, and after it was all over he confronted Falmouth.

'Look here, Falmouth,' he said pugnaciously, 'what's the racket?' Falmouth, having reason to know, and to an extent stand in awe of, the little man, waggled his head darkly. 'Oh, rot!' said Charles rudely, 'don't be so disgustingly mysterious — why aren't we allowed to say these chaps died — ?'

'Have you seen Jessen?' asked the detective.

'I have,' said Charles bitterly, 'and after what I've done for that man; after I've put his big feet on the rungs of culture — '

'Wouldn't he speak?' asked Falmouth innocently.

'He was as close,' said Charles sadly, 'as the inside washer of a vacuum pump.'

'H'm!' the detective was considering. Sooner or later the connection must occur to Charles, and he was the only man who would be likely to surprise Jessen's secret. Better that the journalist should know now.

'If I were you,' said Falmouth quietly, 'I shouldn't worry Jessen; you know what he is, and in what capacity he serves the Government. Come along with me.'

He did not speak a word in reply to the questions Charles put until they passed through the showy portals of Carlby Mansions and a lift had deposited them at the door of the flat.

Falmouth opened the door with a key, and Charles went into the flat at his heels.

He saw the hole in the floor.

'This wasn't mentioned at the inquest,' he said; 'but what's this to do with Jessen?'

He looked up at the detective in perplexity, then a light broke upon him and he whistled.

'Well, I'm — ' he said, then he added softly — 'But what does the Government say to this?'

'The Government,' said Falmouth in his

best official manner, smoothing the nap of his hat the while — 'the Government regard the circumstances as unusual, but they have accepted the situation with great philosophy.'

That night Mr. Long (or Jessen) reappeared at the Guild as though nothing whatever had happened, and addressed his audience for half an hour on the subject of 'Do burglars make good caretakers?'

8

An Incident in the Fight

From what secret place in the metropolis the Woman of Gratz reorganized her forces we shall never know; whence came her strength of purpose and her unbounded energy we can guess. With Starque's death she became virtually and actually the leader of the Red Hundred, and from every corner of Europe came reinforcements of men and money to strengthen her hand and to re-establish the shaking prestige of the most powerful association that Anarchism had ever known.

Great Britain had ever been immune from the active operations of the anarchist. It had been the sanctuary of the revolutionary for centuries, and Anarchism had hesitated to jeopardize the security of refugees by carrying on its propaganda on British soil. That the extremists of the movement had chafed under the restriction is well known, and when the Woman of Gratz openly declared war on England, she was acclaimed enthusiastically.

Then followed perhaps the most extraordinary duels that the world had ever seen. Two rful bodies, both outside the pale of the , fought rapidly, mercilessly, asking no uarter and giving none. And the eerie thing about it all was, that no man saw the agents of either of the combatants. It was as though two spirit forces were engaged in some titanic combat. The police were almost helpless. The fight against the Red Hundred was carried on, almost single-handedly, by the Four Just Men, or, to give them the title with which they signed their famous proclamation, 'The Council of Justice' . . .

Since the days of the Fenian scare, London had never lived under the terror that the Red Hundred inspired. Never a day passed but preparations for some outrage were discovered, the most appalling of which was the attempt on the Tube Railway. If I refer to them as *attempts*, and if the repetition of that word wearies the reader, it is because, thanks to the extraordinary vigilance of the Council of Justice, they were no more.

★　★　★

'This sort of thing cannot go on,' said the Home Secretary petulantly at a meeting of the heads of the police. 'Here we have admittedly the finest police force in the world, and we must needs be under

108

obligation to men for whom warrants exist on a charge of murder!'

The chief commissioner was sufficiently harassed, and was inclined to resent the criticism in the minister's voice.

'We've done everything that can be done, sir,' he said shortly; 'if you think my resignation would help you out of the difficulty — '

'Now for heaven's sake, don't be a fool,' pleaded the Home Secretary, in his best unparliamentary manner. 'Cannot you see — '

'I can see that no harm has been done so far,' said the commissioner doggedly; then he burst forth:

'Look here, sir! our people have very often to employ characters a jolly sight worse than the Four Just Men — if we don't employ them we exploit them. Mean little sneak-thieves, 'narks' they call 'em, old lags, burglars — and once or twice something worse. We are here to protect the public; so long as the public is being protected, nobody can kick — '

'But it is not you who are protecting the public — you get your information — '

'From the Council of Justice, that is so; but where it comes from doesn't matter. Now, listen to me, sir.' He was very earnest and emphasized his remarks with little raps on the desk. 'Get the Prince of the Escorial out of the country,' he said seriously. 'I've got information that the Reds are after his blood. No, I haven't been warned by the Just Men, that's the queer part about it. I've got it straight from a man who's selling me information. I shall see him tonight if they haven't butchered him.'

'But the Prince is our guest.'

'He's been here too long,' said the practical and unsentimental commissioner; 'let him go back to Spain — he's to be married in a month; let him go home and buy his *trousseau* or whatever he buys.'

'Is that a confession that you cannot safeguard him?'

The commissioner looked vexed.

'I could safeguard a child of six or a staid gentleman of sixty, but I cannot be responsible for a young man who insists on seeing London without a guide, who takes solitary motor-car drives, and refuses to give us any information beforehand as to his plans for the day — or if he does, breaks them!'

The minister was pacing the apartment with his head bent in thought.

'As to the Prince of the Escorial,' he said presently, 'advice has already been conveyed to his Highness — from the highest quarter

— to make his departure at an early date. Tonight, indeed, is his last night in London.'

The commissioner of Police made an extravagant demonstration of relief.

'He's going to the Auditorium tonight,' he said, rising. He spoke a little pityingly, and, indeed, the Auditorium, although a very first-class music hall, had a slight reputation. 'I shall have a dozen men in the house and we'll have his motor-car at the stage door at the end of the show.'

That night his Highness arrived promptly at eight o'clock and stood chatting pleasantly with the bare-headed manager in the vestibule. Then he went alone to his box and sat down in the shadow of the red velvet curtain.

Punctually at eight there arrived two other gentlemen, also in evening dress. Antonio Selleni was one and Karl Ollmanns was the other. They were both young men, and before they left the motorcar they completed their arrangement.

'You will occupy the box on the opposite side, but I will endeavour to enter the box. If I succeed — it will be finished. The knife is best,' there was pride in the Italian's tone.

'If I cannot reach him the honour will be yours.' He had the stilted manner of the young Latin. The other man grunted. He replied in halting French.

'Once I shot an egg from between fingers — so,' he said.

They made their entry separately.

In the manager's office, Superintendent Falmouth relieved the tedium of waiting by reading the advertisements in an evening newspaper.

To him came the manager with a message that under no circumstances was his Highness in Box A to be disturbed until the conclusion of the performance.

In the meantime Signor Selleni made a cautious way to Box A. He found the road clear, turned the handle softly, and stepped quickly into the dark interior of the box.

Twenty minutes later Falmouth stood at the back of the dress circle issuing instructions to a subordinate.

'Have a couple of men at the stage door — my God!'

Over the soft music, above the hum of voices, a shot rang out and a woman screamed. From the box opposite the Prince's a thin swirl of smoke floated.

Karl Ollmanns, tired of waiting, had fired at the motionless figure sitting in the shadow of the curtain. Then he walked calmly out of the box into the arms of two breathless detectives.

'A doctor!' shouted Falmouth as he ran.

The door of the Box A was locked, but he broke it open.

A man lay on the floor of the box very still and strangely stiff.

'Why, what — !' began the detective, for the dead man was bound hand and foot.

There was already a crowd at the door of the box, and he heard an authoritative voice demand admittance.

He looked over his shoulder to meet the eye of the commissioner.

'They've killed him, sir,' he said bitterly.

'Whom?' asked the commissioner in perplexity.

'His Highness.'

'His Highness!' the commissioner's eyebrows rose in genuine astonishment. 'Why, the Prince left Charing Cross for the Continent half an hour ago!'

The detective gasped.

'Then who in the name of Fate is this?'

It was M. Menshikoff, who had come in with the commissioner, who answered.

'Antonio Selleni, an anarchist of Milan,' he reported.

★ ★ ★

Carlos Ferdinand Bourbon, Prince of the Escorial, Duke of Buda-Gratz, and heir to three thrones, was married, and his many august cousins scattered throughout Europe had a sense of heartfelt relief.

A prince with admittedly advanced views, an idealist, with Utopian schemes for the regeneration of mankind, and, coming down to the mundane practical side of life, a reckless motor-car driver, an outrageously daring horseman, and possessed of the indifference to public opinion which is equally the equipment of your fool and your truly great man, his marriage had been looked forward to throughout the courts of Europe in the light of an international achievement.

Said his Imperial Majesty of Central Europe to the grizzled chancellor:

'*Te Deums* — you understand, von Hedlitz? In every church.'

'It is a great relief,' said the chancellor, wagging his head thoughtfully.

'Relief!' the Emperor stretched himself as though the relief were physical, 'that young man owes me two years of life. You heard of the London essay?'

The chancellor had heard — indeed, he had heard three or four times — but he was a polite chancellor and listened attentively. His Majesty had the true story-telling faculty, and elaborated the introduction.

'. . . if I am to believe his Highness, he was sitting quietly in his box when the Italian entered. He saw the knife in his hand and half rose to grapple with the intruder. Suddenly, from nowhere in particular, sprang three men, who had the assassin on the floor bound and gagged. You would have thought our Carlos Ferdinand would have made an outcry! But not he! He sat stock still, dividing his attention between the stage and the prostrate man and the leader of this mysterious band of rescuers.'

'The Four Just Men!' put in the chancellor.

'Three, so far as I can gather,' corrected the imperial story-teller. 'Well, it would appear that this leader, in quite a logical calm, matter-of-fact way, suggested that the prince should leave quietly; that his motor-car was at the stage door, that a saloon had been reserved at Charing Cross, a cabin at Dover, and a special train at Calais.'

His Majesty had a trick of rubbing his knee when anything amused him, and this he did now.

'Carl obeyed like a child — which seems the remarkably strange point about the whole proceedings — the captured anarchist was trussed and bound and sat on the chair, and left to his own unpleasant thoughts.'

'And killed,' said the chancellor.

'No, not killed,' corrected the Emperor. 'Part of the story I tell you is his — he told it to the police at the hospital — no, no, not killed — his friend was not the marksman he thought.'

9

The Four v. The Hundred

Some workmen, returning home of an evening and taking a short cut through a field two miles from Catford, saw a man hanging from a tree.

They ran across and found a fashionably dressed gentleman of foreign appearance. One of the labourers cut the rope with his knife, but the man was dead when they cut him down. Beneath the tree was a black bag, to which somebody had affixed a label bearing the warning:

Do not touch — this bag contains explosives: inform the police.

More remarkable still was the luggage label tied to the lapel of the dead man's coat. It ran:

This is Franz Kitsinger, convicted at Prague in 1904, for throwing a bomb: escaped from prison March 17, 1905, was one of the three men responsible for the attempt on the Tower Bridge today. Executed by order of The Council of Justice.

★ ★ ★

'It's a humiliating confession,' said the chief commissioner when they brought the news to him, 'but the presence of these men takes a load off my mind.' But the Red Hundred were grimly persistent.

★ ★ ★

That night a man, smoking a cigar, strolled aimlessly past the policeman on point duty at the corner of Kensington Park Gardens, and walked casually into Ladbroke Square. He strolled on, turned a corner and, crossing a road, he came to where one great garden served for a double row of middle-class houses. The backs of these houses opened on to the square. He looked round and, seeing the coast clear, he clambered over the iron railings and dropped into the big pleasure ground, holding very carefully an object that bulged in his pocket.

He took a leisurely view of the houses before he decided on the victim. The blinds of this particular house were up and the

French windows of the dining-room were open, and he could see the laughing group of young people about the table. There was a birthday party or something of the sort in progress, for there was a great parade of Parthian caps and paper sunbonnets.

The man was evidently satisfied with the possibilities for tragedy, and he took a pace nearer . . .

Two strong arms were about him, arms with muscles like cords of steel.

'Not that way, my friend,' whispered a voice in his ear . . .

The man showed his teeth in a dreadful grin.

★ ★ ★

The sergeant on duty at Notting Hill Gate Station received a note at the hands of a grimy urchin, who for days afterwards maintained a position of enviable notoriety.

'A gentleman told me to bring this,' he said.

The sergeant looked at the small boy sternly and asked him if he ever washed his face. Then he read the letter:

The second man of the three concerned in the attempt to blow up the Tower

Bridge will be found in the garden of Maidham Crescent, under the laurel bushes, opposite No. 72.

It was signed 'The Council of Justice'.

★ ★ ★

The commissioner was sitting over his coffee at the Ritz, when they brought him the news. Falmouth was a deferential guest, and the chief passed him the note without comment.

'This is going to settle the Red Hundred,' said Falmouth. 'These people are fighting them with their own weapons — assassination with assassination, terror with terror. Where do we come in?'

'We come in at the end,' said the commissioner, choosing his words with great niceness, 'to clean up the mess, and take any scraps of credit that are going' — he paused and shook his head. 'I hope — I should be sorry — ' he began.

'So should I,' said the detective sincerely, for he knew that his chief was concerned for the ultimate safety of the men whose arrest it was his duty to effect. The commissioner's brows were wrinkled thoughtfully.

'Two,' he said musingly; 'now, how on

earth do the Four Just Men know the number in this — and how did they track them down — and who is the third? — heavens! one could go on asking questions the whole of the night!'

* * *

On one point the commissioner might have been informed earlier in the evening — he was not told until three o'clock the next morning. The third man was Von Dunop. Ignorant of the fate of his fellow-terrorists, he sallied forth to complete the day notably.

The crowd at a theatre door started a train of thought, but he rejected that outlet to ambition. It was too public, and the chance of escape was nil. These British audiences did not lose their heads so quickly; they refused to be confounded by noise and smoke, and a writhing figure here and there. Von Dunop was no exponent of the Glory of Death school. He greatly desired glory, but the smaller the risk, the greater the glory. This was his code.

He stood for a moment outside the Hotel Ritz. A party of diners were leaving, and motor-cars were being steered up to carry these accursed plutocrats to the theatre. One soldierly-looking gentleman, with a grey moustache, and attended by a quiet, observant, clean-shaven man, interested the anarchist. He and the soldier exchanged glances.

'Who the dickens was that?' asked the commissioner as he stepped into the taxi. 'I seem to know his face.'

'I have seen him before,' said Falmouth. 'I won't go with you, sir — I've a little business to do in this part of the world.'

Thereafter Von Dunop was not permitted to enjoy his walk in solitude, for, unknown to him, a man 'picked him up' and followed him throughout the evening. And as the hour grew later, that one man became two, at eleven o'clock he became three, and at quarter to twelve, when Von Dunop had finally fixed upon the scene and scope of his exploit, he turned from Park Lane into Brook Street to discover, to his annoyance, quite a number of people within call. Yet he suspected nothing. He did not suspect the night wanderer mooching along the curb with downcast eyes, seeking the gutter for the stray cigar end; nor the two loudly talking men in suits of violet check who wrangled as they walked concerning the relative merits of the favourites for the Derby; nor the commission-aire trudging home with his bag in his hand and a pipe in his mouth, nor the clean-shaven man in evening dress.

The Home Secretary had a house in Berkeley Square. Von Dunop knew the number very well. He slackened pace to allow the man in evening dress to pass. The slow-moving taxi that was fifty yards away he must risk. This taxi had been his constant attendant during the last hour, but he did not know it.

He dipped his hand into his overcoat pocket and drew forth the machine. It was one of Culveri's masterpieces and, to an extent, experimental — that much the master had warned him in a letter that bore the date-mark 'Riga.' He felt with his thumb for the tiny key that set the machine and pushed it.

Then he slipped into the doorway of No. 196 and placed the bomb. It was done in a second, and so far as he could tell no man had seen him leave the pathway and he was back again on the sidewalk very quickly. But as he stepped back, he heard a shout and a man darted across the road, calling on him to surrender. From the left two men were running, and he saw the man in evening dress blowing a whistle.

He was caught; he knew it. There was a chance of escape — the other end of the street was clear — he turned and ran like the wind. He could hear his pursuers pattering along behind him. His ear, alert to every phase of the chase, heard one pair of feet check and spring up the steps of 196. He glanced round. They were gaining on him, and he turned suddenly and fired three times. Somebody fell; he saw that much. Then right ahead of him a tall policeman sprang from the shadows and clasped him round the waist.

'Hold that man!' shouted Falmouth, running up. Blowing hard came the night wanderer, a ragged object but skilful, and he had Von Dunop handcuffed in a trice.

It was he who noticed the limpness of the prisoner.

'Hullo!' he said, then held out his hand. 'Show a light here.'

There were half a dozen policemen and the inevitable crowd on the spot by now, and the rays of the bull's-eye focused on the detective's hand. It was red with blood. Falmouth seized a lantern and flashed it on the man's face.

There was no need to look farther. He was dead — dead with the inevitable label affixed to the handle of the knife that killed him.

Falmouth rapped out an oath.

'It is incredible; it is impossible! he was running till the constable caught him, and he

124

has not been out of our hands! Where is the officer who held him?'

Nobody answered, certainly not the tall policeman, who was at that moment being driven eastward, making a rapid change into the conventional evening costume of an English gentleman.

10

The Trial

To fathom the mind of the Woman of Gratz is
no easy task, and one not to be lightly
undertaken. Remembering her obscure beginning, the bare-legged child drinking in revolutionary
talk in the Transylvanian kitchen, and the
development of her intellect along unconven-
tional lines — remembering, also, that early in
life she made acquaintance with the extreme
problems of life and death in their least attrac-
tive forms, and that the proportion of things
had been grossly distorted by her teachers,
you may arrive at a point where your vacillat-
ing judgement hesitates between blame and
pity.

I would believe that the power of
introspection had no real place in her mental
equipment, else how can we explain her
attitude towards the man whom she had once
defied and reconcile those outbursts of hers
wherein she called for his death, for his
terrible punishment, wherein, too, she allowed
herself the rare luxury of unrestrained speech,
how can we reconcile these tantrums with the

fact that this man's voice filled her thoughts day and night, the recollection of this man's eyes through his mask followed her every movement, till the image of him became an obsession?

It may be that I have no knowledge of women and their ways (there is no subtle smugness in the doubt I express) and that her inconsistency was general to her sex. It must not be imagined that she had spared either trouble or money to secure the extermination of her enemies, and the enemies of the Red Hundred. She had described them, as well as she could, after her first meeting, and the sketches made under her instruction had been circulated by the officers of the Reds.

Sitting near the window of her house, she mused, lulled by the ceaseless hum of traffic in the street below, and half dozing.

The turning of the door-handle woke her from her dreams.

It was Schmidt, the unspeakable Schmidt, all perspiration and excitement. His round coarse face glowed with it, and he could scarcely bring his voice to tell the news.

'We have him! We have him!' he cried in glee, and snapped his fingers. 'Oh, the good news! — I am the first! Nobody has been, Little Friend? I have run and have taken taxis — '

'You have — whom?' she asked.

'The man — one of the men' he said, 'who killed Starque and Francois, and — '

'Which — which man?' she said harshly.

He fumbled in his pocket and pulled out a discoloured sketch.

'Oh!' she said, it could not be the man whom she had defied, 'Why, why?' she asked stormily, 'Why only this man? Why not the others — why not the leader? — Have they caught him and lost him?'

Chagrin and astonishment sat on Schmidt's round face. His disappointment was almost comic.

'But, Little Mother!' he said, crestfallen and bewildered, 'this is one — we did not hope even for one and — '

The storm passed over.

'Yes, yes,' she said wearily, 'one — even one is good. They shall learn that the Red Hundred can still strike — this leader shall know — This man shall have a death,' she said, looking at Schmidt 'worthy of his importance. Tell me how he was captured.'

'It was the picture,' said the eager Schmidt, 'the picture you had drawn. One of our comrades thought he recognized him and followed him to his house.'

'He shall be tried — tonight,' and she spent the day anticipating her triumph.

Conspirators do not always choose dark arches for their plottings. The Red Hundred especially were notorious for the likeliness of their rendezvous. They went to nature for a precedent, and as she endows the tiger with stripes that are undistinguishable from the jungle grass, so the Red Hundred would choose for their meetings such a place where meetings were usually held.

It was in the Lodge Room of the Pride of Millwall, AOSA — which may be amplified as the Associated Order of the Sons of Abstinence — that the trial took place. The financial position of the Pride of Millwall was not strong. An unusual epidemic of temperate seafaring men had called the Lodge into being, the influx of capital from eccentric bequests had built the tiny hall, and since the fiasco attending the first meeting of the League of London, much of its public business had been skilfully conducted in these riverside premises. It had been raided by the police during the days of terror, but nothing of an incriminating character had been discovered. Because of the success with which the open policy had been pursued the Woman of Gratz preferred to take the risk of an open trial in a hall liable to police raid.

The man must be so guarded that escape was impossible. Messengers sped in every direction to carry out her instruction. There was a rapid summoning of leaders of the movement, the choice of the place of trial, the preparation for a ceremony which was governed by well-established precedent, and the arrangement of the properties which played so effective a part in the trials of the Hundred.

In the black-draped chamber of trial the Woman of Gratz found a full company. Maliscrivona, Tchezki, Vellantini, De Romans, to name a few who were there sitting altogether side by side on the low forms, and they buzzed a welcome as she walked into the room and took her seat at the higher place. She glanced round the faces, bestowing a nod here and a glance of recognition there. She remembered the last time she had made an appearance before the rank and file of the movement. She missed many faces that had turned to her in those days: Starque, Francois, Kitsinger — dead at the hands of the Four Just Men. It fitted her mood to remember that tonight she would judge one who had at least helped in the slaying of Starque.

Abruptly she rose. Lately she had had few opportunities for the display of that oratory which was once her sole title to consideration in the councils of the Red Hundred. Her powers of organization had come to be respected later. She felt the want of practice as she began speaking. She found herself hesitating for words, and once she felt her illustrations were crude. But she gathered confidence as she proceeded and she felt the responsive thrill of a fascinated audience.

It was the story of the campaign that she told. Much of it we know; the story from the point of view of the Reds may be guessed. She finished her speech by recounting the capture of the enemy.

'Tonight we aim a blow at these enemies of progress; if they have been merciless, let us show them that the Red Hundred is not to be outdone in ferocity. As they struck, so let us strike — and, in striking, read a lesson to the men who killed our comrades, that they, nor the world, will ever forget.'

There was no cheering as she finished — that had been the order — but a hum of words as they flung their tributes of words at her feet — a ruck of incoherent phrases of praise and adoration.

Then two men led in the prisoner.

He was calm and interested, throwing out his square chin resolutely when the first words of the charge were called and twiddling the fingers of his bound hands absently.

He met the scowling faces turned to him serenely, but as they proceeded with the indictment, he grew attentive, bending his head to catch the words.

Once he interrupted.

'I cannot quite understand that,' he said in fluent Russian, 'my knowledge of German is limited.'

'What is your nationality?' demanded the woman.

'English,' he replied.

'Do you speak French?' she asked.

'I am learning,' he said naively, and smiled.

'You speak Russian,' she said. Her conversation was carried on in that tongue.

'Yes,' he said simply; 'I was there for many years.'

After this, the sum of his transgressions were pronounced in a language he understood. Once or twice as the reader proceeded — it was Ivan Oranvitch who read — the man smiled.

The Woman of Gratz recognized him instantly as the fourth of the party that gathered about her door the day Bartholomew was murdered. Formally she asked him what he had to say before he was condemned.

He smiled again.

'I am not one of the Four Just Men,' he

said; 'whoever says I am — lies.'

'And is that all you have to say?' she asked scornfully.

'That is all,' was his calm reply.

'Do you deny that you helped slay our comrade Starque?'

'I do not deny it,' he said easily, 'I did not help — I killed him.'

'Ah!' the exclamation came simultaneously from every throat.

'Do you deny that you have killed many of the Red Hundred?'

He paused before he answered.

'As to the Red Hundred — I do not know; but I have killed many people.' He spoke with the grave air of a man filled with a sense of responsibility, and again the exclamatory hum ran through the hall. Yet, the Woman of Gratz had a growing sense of unrest in spite of the success of the examination.

'You have said you were in Russia — did men fall to your hand there?'

He nodded.

'And in England?'

'Also in England,' he said.

'What is your name?' she asked. By an oversight it was a question — she had not put before.

The man shrugged his shoulders.

'Does it matter?' he asked. A thought

struck her. In the hall she had seen Magnus the Jew. He had lived for many years in England, and she beckoned him.

'Of what class is this man?' she asked in a whisper.

'Of the lower orders,' he replied; 'it is astounding — did you not notice when — no, you did not see his capture. But he spoke like a man of the streets, dropping his aspirates.'

He saw she looked puzzled and explained.

'It is a trick of the order — just as the Moujik says . . . ' he treated her to a specimen of colloquial Russian.

'What is your name?' she asked again.

He looked at her slyly.

'In Russia they called me Father Kopab . . . '

The majority of those who were present were Russian, and at the word they sprang to their feet, shrinking back with ashen faces, as though they feared contact with the man who stood bound and helpless in the middle of the room.

The Woman of Gratz had risen with the rest. Her lips quivered and her wide open eyes spoke her momentary terror.

'I killed Starque,' he went on, 'by authority. Francois also. Some day' — he looked leisurely about the room — 'I shall also — '

'Stop!' she cried, and then:

'Release him,' she said, and, wonderingly,

134

Schmidt cut the bonds that bound him. He stretched himself.

'When you took me,' he said, 'I had a book; you will understand that here in England I find — forgetfulness in books — and I, who have seen so much suffering and want caused through departure from the law, am striving as hard for the regeneration of mankind as you — but differently.'

Somebody handed him a book.

He looked at it, nodded, and slipped it into his pocket.

'Farewell,' he said as he turned to the open door.

'In God's name!' said the Woman of Gratz, trembling, 'go in peace, Little Father.'

And the man Jessen, sometime headsman to the Supreme Council, and latterly public executioner of England, walked out, no man barring his exit.

★ ★ ★

The power of the Red Hundred was broken. This much Falmouth knew. He kept an ever-vigilant band of men on duty at the great termini of London, and to these were attached the members of a dozen secret police forces of Europe. Day by day, there was the same report to make. Such and such a man, whose very presence in London had been unsuspected, had left via Harwich. So-and-so, surprisingly sprung from nowhere, had gone by the eleven o'clock train from Victoria; by the Hull and Stockholm route twenty had gone in one day, and there were others who made Liverpool, Glasgow, and Newcastle their port of embarkation.

I think that it was only then that Scotland Yard realized the strength of the force that had lain inert in the metropolis, or appreciated the possibilities for destruction that had been to hand in the days of the Terror.

Certainly every batch of names that appeared on the commissioner's desk made him more thoughtful than ever.

'Arrest them!' he said in horror when the suggestion was made. 'Arrest them! Look here, have you ever seen driver ants attack a house in Africa? Marching in, in endless battalions at midnight and clearing out everything living from chickens to beetles? Have you ever seen them re-form in the morning and go marching home again? You wouldn't think of arresting 'em, would you? No, you'd just sit down quietly out of their reach and be happy when the last little red leg has disappeared round the corner!'

Those who knew the Red Hundred best were heartily in accord with his philosophy.

'They caught Jessen,' reported Falmouth. 'Oh!' said the commissioner.

'When he disclosed his identity, they got rid of him quick.'

'I've often wondered why the Four Just Men didn't do the business of Starque themselves,' mused the commissioner.

'It was rather rum,' admitted Falmouth, 'but Starque was a man under sentence, as also was Francois. By some means they got hold of the original warrants, and it was on these that Jessen — did what he did.'

The commissioner nodded. 'And now,' he asked, 'what about them?'

Falmouth had expected this question sooner or later.

'Do you suggest that we should catch them, sir?' he asked with thinly veiled sarcasm. 'Because if you do, sir, I have only to remind you that we've been trying to do that for some years.' The chief commissioner frowned.

'It's a remarkable thing,' he said, 'that as soon as we get a situation such as — the Red Hundred scare and the Four Just Men scare, for instance, we're completely at sea, and that's what the papers will say. It doesn't sound creditable, but it's so.'

'I place the superintendent's defence of Scotland Yard on record *in extenso*.

'What the papers say,' said Falmouth, 'never keeps me awake at night. Nobody's quite got the hang of the police force in this country — certainly the writing people haven't.

'There are two ways of writing about the police, sir. One way is to deal with them in the newspaper fashion with the headline 'Another Police Blunder' or 'The Police and The Public,' and the other way is to deal with them in the magazine style, which is to show them as softies on the wrong scent, whilst an ornamental civilian is showing them their business, or as mysterious people with false beards who pop up at the psychological moment, and say in a loud voice, 'In the name of the Law, I arrest you!'

'Well, I don't mind admitting that I know neither kind. I've been a police officer for twenty-three years, and the only assistance I've had from a civilian was from a man named Blackie, who helped me to find the body of a woman that had disappeared. I was rather prejudiced against him, but I don't mind admitting that he was pretty smart and followed his clues with remarkable ingenuity.

'The day we found the body I said to him: 'Mr. Blackie, you have given me a great deal of information about this woman's movements — in fact, you know a great deal more than you ought to know — so I shall take you into custody on the suspicion of having caused her death.' Before he died he made a full confession, and ever since then I have always been pleased to take as much advice and help from outside as I could get.

'When people sometimes ask me about the cleverness of Scotland Yard, I can't tell 'em tales such as you read about. I've had murderers, anarchists, burglars, and average low-down people to deal with, but they have mostly done their work in a commonplace way and bolted. And as soon as they have bolted, we've employed fairly commonplace methods and brought 'em back.

'If you ask me whether I've been in dreadful danger, when arresting desperate murderers and criminals, I say 'No.'

'When your average criminal finds himself cornered, he says, 'All right, Mr. Falmouth; it's a cop,' and goes quietly.

'Crime and criminals run in grooves. They're hardy annuals with perennial methods. Extraordinary circumstances baffle the police as they baffle other folks. You can't run a business on business lines and be absolutely prepared for anything that turns up. Whiteley's will supply you with a flea or an elephant, but if a woman asked a shop girl to hold her baby whilst she went into the tinned meat department, the girl and the manager and the whole system would be floored, because there is no provision for holding babies. And if a Manchester goods merchant, unrolling his stuff, came upon a snake lying all snug in the bale, he'd be floored too, because natural history isn't part of their business training, and they wouldn't be quite sure whether it was a big worm or a boa constrictor.'

The commissioner was amused.

'You've an altogether unexpected sense of humour,' he said, 'and the moral is — '

'That the unexpected always floors you, whether it's humour or crime,' said Falmouth, and went away fairly pleased with himself.

$$\star \quad \star \quad \star$$

In his room he found a waiting messenger.

'A lady to see you, sir.'

'Who is it?' he asked in surprise.

The messenger handed him a slip of paper and when he read it he whistled.

'The unexpected, by — ! Show her up.'

On the paper was written — 'The Woman of Gratz . . . '

11

Manfred

Manfred sat alone in his Lewisham house — he was known to the old lady who was his caretaker as 'a foreign gentleman in the music line' — and in the subdued light of the shaded lamp, he looked tired. A book lay on the table near at hand, and a silver coffee-service and an empty coffee-cup stood on the stool by his side. Reaction he felt. This strange man had set himself to a task that was never ending. The destruction of the forces of the Red Hundred was the end of a fight that cleared the ground for the commencement of another — but physically he was weary.

Gonsalez had left that morning for Paris, Poiccart went by the afternoon train, and he was to join them tomorrow.

The strain of the fight had told on them, all three. Financially, the cost of the war had been heavy, but that strain they could stand better than any other, for had they not the fortune of — Courtlander; in case of need they knew their man.

All the world had been searched before

they — the first Four — had come together — Manfred, Gonsalez, Poiccart, and the man who slept eternally in the flower-grown grave at Bordeaux. As men taking the oaths of priesthood they lived down the passions and frets of life. Each man was an open book to the other, speaking his most secret thought in the faith of sympathy, one dominating thought controlling them all.

They had made the name of the Four Just Men famous or infamous (according to your point of reckoning) throughout the civilized world. They came as a new force into public and private life. There were men, free of the law, who worked misery on their fellows; dreadful human ghouls fattening on the bodies and souls of the innocent and helpless; great magnates calling the law to their aid, or pushing it aside as circumstances demanded. All these became amenable to a new law, a new tribunal. There had grown into being systems which defied correction; corporations beyond chastisement; individuals protected by cunningly drawn legislation, and others who knew to an inch the scope of toleration. In the name of justice, these men struck swiftly, dispassionately, mercilessly. The great swindler, the *procureur*, the suborner of witnesses, the briber of juries — they died.

There was no gradation of punishment: a

warning, a second warning — then death.

Thus their name became a symbol, at which the evildoer went tremblingly about his work, dreading the warning and ready in most cases to heed it. Life became a sweeter, a more wholesome thing for many men who found the thin greenish-grey envelope on their breakfast-table in the morning; but others persisted on their way, loudly invoking the law, which in spirit, if not in letter, they had outraged. The end was very sure, and I do not know of one man who escaped the consequence.

Speculating on their identity, the police of the world decided unanimously upon two points. The first was that these men were enormously rich — as indeed they were, and the second that one or two of them were no mean scientists — that also was true. Of the fourth man who had joined them recently, speculation took a wider turn. Manfred smiled as he thought of this fourth member, of his honesty, his splendid qualities of heart and brain, his enthusiasm, and his proneness to 'lapse from the balance' — Gonsalez coined the phrase. It was an affectionate smile. The fourth man was no longer of the brotherhood; he had gone, the work being completed, and there were other reasons.

So Manfred was musing, till the little clock

on the mantelpiece chimed ten, then he lit the spirit-kettle and brewed another cup of coffee. Thus engaged, he heard the far-away tinkle of a bell and the opening of a door. Then a murmur of voices and two steps on the stairs. He did not expect visitors, but he was always prepared for them at any hour.

'Come in,' he said, in answer to the knock; he recognized the apologetic rap of his housekeeper.

'A lady — a foreign lady to see you.'

'Show her in, please,' he said courteously.

He was busy with the kettle when she came in. He did not look up, nor did he ask who it was. His housekeeper stood a moment uncertain on the threshold, then went out, leaving them together.

'You will excuse me a moment,' he said. 'Please sit down.'

He poured out the coffee with a steady hand, walked to his desk, sorted a number of letters, tossed them into the grate, and stood for a moment watching them burn, then looked at her.

Taking no notice of his invitation, the girl stood waiting at ease, one hand on her hip, the other hanging loosely.

'Won't you sit down?' he asked again.

'I prefer to stand,' she said shortly.

'Then you are not so tired as I am,' he said,

and sank back into the depths of his chair.

She did not reply, and for a few seconds neither spoke.

'Has the Woman of Gratz forgotten that she is an orator?' he said banteringly. It seemed to him that there was in those eyes of hers a great yearning, and he changed his tone.

'Sit down, Maria,' he said gently. He saw the flush that rose to her cheek, and mistook its significance.

'No, no!' he hastened to rectify an impression. 'I am serious now, I am not gibing — why have you not gone with the others?'

'I have work to do,' she said.

He stretched out his hands in a gesture of weariness.

'Work, work, work!' he said with a bitter smile, 'isn't the work finished? Isn't there an end to this work of yours?'

'The end is at hand,' she said, and looked at him strangely.

'Sit down,' he commanded, and she took the nearest chair and watched him.

Then she broke the silence.

'What are you?' she asked, with a note of irritation. 'Who gave authority?'

He laughed.

'What am I — just a man, Maria. Authority? As you understand it — none.'

She was thoughtful for a moment.

'You have not asked me why I have come,' she said.

'I have not asked myself — yet it seems natural that you and I should meet again — to part.'

'What do they call you — your friends?' she asked suddenly. 'Do they say 'the man with the beard,' or 'the tall man' — did any woman ever nurse you and call you by name?'

A shadow passed over his face for a second.

'Yes,' he said quietly; 'I have told you I am human; neither devil nor demi-god, no product of sea-foam or witches' cauldron,' he smiled, 'but a son of earthly parents — and men call me George Manfred.'

'George,' she repeated as though learning a lesson. 'George Manfred.' She looked at him long and earnestly, and frowned.

'What is it you see that displeases you?' he asked.

'Nothing,' she said quickly, 'only I am — I cannot understand — you are different — '

'From what you expected.' She bent her head. 'You expected me to air a triumph. To place myself in defence?' She nodded again.

'No, no,' he went on, 'that is finished. I do not pursue a victory — I am satisfied that the power of your friends is shattered. I dissociate you from the humiliation of their defeat.'

146

'I am no better nor worse than they,' she said defiantly.

'You will be better when the madness passes,' he said gravely, 'when you realize that your young life was not meant for the dreadful sacrifice of anarchy.'

He leant over and took her listless hand and held it between his palms.

'Child, you must leave this work,' he said softly, 'forget the nightmare of your past — put it out of your mind, so that you will come to believe that the Red Hundred never existed.'

She did not draw away her hand, nor did she attempt to check the tears that came to her eyes. Something had entered her soul — an influence that was beyond all description or definition. A wonderful element that had dissolved the thing of granite and steel, that she had fondly thought was her heart, and left her weak and shaking in the process.

'Maria, if you ever knew a mother's love' — how soft his voice was — 'think of that: have you ever realized what your tiny life was to her — how she planned and thought and suffered for you — and to what end? That the hands she kissed should be set against men's lives! Did she pray to God that He might keep you strong in health and pure in soul — only that His gifts should prove a curse to

His beautiful world?'

With the tenderness of a father he drew her to him, till she was on her knees before him and her weeping face was pressed closely against him.

His strong arms were about her, and his hand smoothed her hair.

'I am a wicked woman,' she sobbed, 'a wicked, wicked woman.'

'Hush,' he said sadly; 'do not let us take our conception of wickedness from our deeds, but from our intentions, however mistaken, however much they traverse the written law.'

But her sobbing grew wilder, and she clutched him as though in fear that he would leave her.

He talked to her as though she were a frightened child, chiding her, laughing at her in gentle raillery, and she grew calmer and presently lifted her stained face to his.

'Listen,' she said; 'I — I — oh, I cannot, I cannot say it.' And she buried her face on her breast.

Then with an effort she raised her head again.

'If I asked you — if I begged you to do something for me — would you?'

He looked into her eyes, smiling.

'You have done many things — you have

killed — yes — yes, let me say it — I know I am hurting you, but let me finish.'

'Yes,' he said simply; 'I have killed.'

'Have you — pitied as you killed?'

He shook his head.

'Yet you would,' she went on, and her distress moved him, 'you would if you thought that you could kill a body and save a soul.'

He shook his head again.

'Yes, yes,' she whispered, and tried to speak. Twice she attempted to frame the words, and twice she failed. Then she pushed herself slowly backwards with her hands at his chest, and crouched before him with parted lips and heaving bosom.

'Kill me,' she breathed, 'for I have betrayed you to the police.'

Still he made no sign, sitting there all huddled in the big chair, as though every muscle of his body had relaxed.

'Do you hear?' she cried fiercely. 'I have betrayed you because — I think — I love you — but I — I did not know it — I did not know it! I hated you so that I pitied you — and always I thought of you!'

She knew by the look of pain in his eyes what her words had cost him.

Somehow she divined that the betrayal hurt least.

'I have never said it to myself,' she

149

whispered; 'I have never thought it in my most secret thoughts — yet it was there, there all the time, waiting for expression — and I am happier, though you die, and though every hour of my life be a lifetime of pain, I am happier that I have said it, happier than I thought I could ever be.

'I have wondered why I remembered you, and why I thought of you, and why you came into my every dream. I thought it was because I hated you, because I wanted to kill you, and to hold you at my mercy — but I know now, I know now.'

She rocked from side to side, clasping her hands in the intensity of her passion.

'You do not speak?' she cried. 'Do you not understand, beloved? I have handed you over to the police, because — O God! because I love you! It must be that I do!'

He leant forward and held out his hands and she came to him half swooning.

'Marie, child,' he murmured, and she saw how pale he was, 'we are strangely placed, you and I to talk of love. You must forget this, little girl; let this be the waking point of your bad dream; go forth into the new life — into a life where flowers are, and birds sing, and where rest and peace is.'

She had no thought now save for his danger.

'They are below,' she moaned. 'I brought them here — I guided them.'

He smiled into her face.

'I knew,' he said.

She looked at him incredulously.

'You knew,' she said, slowly.

'Yes — when you came' — he pointed to the heap of burnt papers in the grate — 'I knew.'

He walked to the window and looked out. What he saw satisfied him.

He came back to where she still crouched on the floor and lifted her to her feet.

She stood unsteadily, but his arm supported her. He was listening, he heard the door open below.

'You must not think of me,' he said again.

She shook her head helplessly, and her lips quivered.

'God bless you and help you,' he said reverently, and kissed her.

Then he turned to meet Falmouth.

'George Manfred,' said the officer, and looked at the girl in perplexity.

'That is my name,' said Manfred quietly. 'You are Inspector Falmouth.'

'Superintendent,' corrected the other.

'I'm sorry,' said Manfred.

'I shall take you into custody,' said Falmouth, 'on suspicion of being a member of an organization known as the Four Just Men, and accordingly concerned in the following crimes — '

'I will excuse you the recital,' said Manfred pleasantly, and held out his hands. For the first time in his life he felt the cold contact of steel at his wrists.

The man who snapped the handcuffs on was nervous and bungled, and Manfred, after an interested glance at the gyves, lifted his hands.

'This is not quite fastened,' he said.

Then as they closed round him, he half turned toward the girl and smiled.

'Who knows how bright are the days in store for us both?' he said softly.

Then they took him away.

12

In Wandsworth Gaol

Charles Garrett, admirable journalist, had written the last line of a humorous description of a local concert at which a cabinet minister had sung pathetic ballads. Charles wrote with difficulty, for the situation had been of itself so funny, that extracting its hidden humours was a more than ordinarily heartbreaking thing. But he had finished and the thick batch of copy lay on the chief sub-editor's desk — Charles wrote on an average six words to a folio, and a half a column story from his pen bulked like a three-volume novel.

Charles stopped to threaten an office-boy who had misdirected a letter, strolled into various quiet offices to 'see who was there' and with his raincoat on his arm, and his stick in his hand, stopped at the end of his wanderings before the chattering tape machine. He looked through the glass box that shielded the mechanism, and was interested in a message from Teheran in the course of transmission.

... at early date. Grand Vizier has informed Exchange Correspondent that the construction of line will be pushed forward ...

The tape stopped its stuttering and buzzed excitedly, then came a succession of quick jerks that cleared away the uncompleted message. Then ' . . . the leader of the Four Just Men was arrested in London tonight,' said the tape, and Charles broke for the editor's room.

He flung open the door without ceremony, and repeated the story the little machine had told.

The grey chief received the news quietly, and the orders he gave in the next five minutes inconvenienced some twenty or thirty unoffending people.

The construction of the 'story' of the Four Just Men, began at the lower rung of the intellectual ladder.

'You boy! get half a dozen taxicabs here quick . . . Poynter, 'phone the reporters in . . . get the Lambs Club on the 'phone and see if O'Mahony or any other of our bright youths are there . . . There are five columns about the Four Just Men standing in the gallery, get it pulled up, Mr. Short . . . pictures — h'm . . . yet wire Massonni to get down to the police station and see if he can find a policeman who'll give him material for a sketch . . . Off you go, Charles, and get the story.'

There was no flurry, no rush; it was for all the world like the scene on a modern battleship when 'clear lower deck for action' had sounded. Two hours to get the story into the paper was ample, and there was no need for the whip.

★　★　★

Later, with the remorseless hands of the clock moving on, taxi after taxi flew up to the great newspaper office, discharging alert young men who literally leapt into the building. Later, with waiting operators sitting tensely before the keyboards of the linotypes, came Charles Garrett doing notable things with a stump of pencil and a ream of thin copy paper.

It was the *Megaphone* that shone splendidly amidst its journalistic fellows, with pages — I quote the envenomed opinion of the news editor of the *Mercury* — that 'shouted like the checks on a bookmaker's waistcoat.'

It was the *Megaphone* that fed the fires of public interest, and was mainly responsible for the huge crowds that gathered outside Greenwich Police Court, and overflowed in dense masses to the foot of Blackheath Hill, whilst Manfred underwent his preliminary inquiries.

'George Manfred, aged 39, of no occupation, residing at Hill Crest Lodge, St John's.' In this prosaic manner he was introduced to the world.

He made a striking figure in the steel-railed dock. A chair was placed for him, and he was guarded as few prisoners had been guarded. A special cell had been prepared for his reception, and departing from established custom, extra warders were detailed to watch him. Falmouth took no risks.

The charge that had been framed had to do with no well-known case. Many years before, one Samuel Lipski, a notorious East End sweater, had been found dead with the stereotyped announcement that he had fallen to the justice of the Four. Upon this the Treasury founded its case for the prosecution — a case which had been very thoroughly and convincingly prepared, and pigeon-holed against such time as arrest should overtake one or the other of the Four Just Men.

Reading over the thousands of newspaper cuttings dealing with the preliminary examination and trial of Manfred, I am struck with the absence of any startling feature, such as one might expect to find in a great state trial of this description. Summarizing the evidence that was given at the police court, one might arrange the 'parts' of the dozen or so commonplace witnesses so that they read:

A policeman: 'I found the body.'

An inspector: 'I read the label.'

A doctor: 'I pronounced him dead.'

An only man with a slight squint and broken English: 'This man Lipski, I known him, he were a goot man and make the business wit the head, ker-vick.'

And the like.

Manfred refused to plead 'guilty' or 'not guilty.' He spoke only once during the police court proceedings, and then only when the formal question had been put to him.

'I am prepared to abide by the result of my trial,' he said clearly, 'and it cannot matter much one way or the other whether I plead guilty or not guilty.'

'I will enter your plea as 'not guilty,'' said the magistrate.

Manfred bowed.

'That is at your worship's discretion,' he said.

On the seventh of June he was formally committed for trial. He had a short interview with Falmouth before he was removed from the police-court cells.

Falmouth would have found it difficult to analyse his feelings towards this man. He scarcely knew himself whether he was glad or sorry that fate had thrown the redoubtable leader into his hands.

His attitude to Manfred was that of a subordinate to a superior, and that attitude he would have found hardest to explain.

When the cell door was opened to admit the detective, Manfred was reading. He rose with a cheery smile to greet his visitor.

'Well, Mr. Falmouth,' he said lightly, 'we enter upon the second and more serious act of the drama.'

'I don't know whether I'm glad or sorry,' said Falmouth bluntly.

'You ought to be glad,' said Manfred with his quizzical smile. 'For you've vindicated — '

'Yes, I know all about that,' said Falmouth dryly, 'but it's the other pan I hate.'

'You mean — ?'

Manfred did not complete the question.

'I do — it's a hanging job, Mr. Manfred, and that is the hateful business after the wonderful work you've done for the country.'

Manfred threw back his head, and laughed in unrestrained amusement.

'Oh, it's nothing to laugh about,' said the plain-spoken detective, 'you are against a bad

158

proposition — the Home Secretary is a cousin of Ramon's, and he hates the very name of the Four Just Men.'

'Yet I may laugh,' said Manfred calmly, 'for I shall escape.'

There was no boastfulness in the speech, but a quiet assurance that had the effect of nettling the other.

'Oh, you will, will you?' he said grimly. 'Well, we shall see.'

There was no escape for Manfred in the dozen yards or so between his cell door and the prison van. He was manacled to two warders, and a double line of policemen formed an avenue through which he was marched. Not from the van itself that moved in a solid phalanx of mounted men with drawn swords. Nor from the gloomy portals of Wandsworth Gaol where silent, uniformed men closed round him and took him to the triple-locked cell.

Once in the night, as he slept, he was awakened by the sound of the changing guard, and this amused him.

* * *

If one had the space to write, one could compile a whole book concerning Manfred's life during the weeks he lay in gaol awaiting

159

trial. He had his visitors. Unusual laxity was allowed in this respect. Falmouth hoped to find the other two men. He generously confessed his hope to Manfred.

'You may make your mind easy on that point,' said Manfred; 'they will not come.'

Falmouth believed him.

'If you were an ordinary criminal, Mr. Manfred,' he said smilingly, 'I should hint the possibilities of King's evidence, but I won't insult you.'

Manfred's reply staggered him.

'Of course not,' he said with an air of innocence; 'if they were arrested, who on earth would arrange my escape?'

The Woman of Gratz did not come to see him, and he was glad.

He had his daily visits from the governor, and found him charmingly agreeable. They talked of countries known to both, of people whom each knew equally well, and tacitly avoided forbidden subjects. Only —

'I hear you are going to escape?' said the governor, as he concluded one of these visits. He was a largely built man, sometime Major of Marine Artillery, and he took life seriously. Therefore he did not share Falmouth's view of the projected escape as being an ill-timed jest.

'Yes,' replied Manfred.

160

'From here?'

Manfred shook his head solemnly.

'The details have not yet been arranged,' he said with admirable gravity. The governor frowned.

'I don't believe you're trying to pull my leg — it's too devilishly serious a matter to joke about — but it would be an awkward thing for me if you got away.' He was of the prisoner's own caste and he had supreme faith in the word of the man who discussed prison-breaking so light-heartedly.

'That I realize,' said Manfred with a little show of deference, 'and I shall accordingly arrange my plans, so that the blame shall be equally distributed.'

The governor, still frowning thoughtfully, left the cell. He came back in a few minutes.

'By the way, Manfred,' he said, 'I forgot to tell you that you'll get a visit from the chaplain. He's a very decent young fellow, and I know I needn't ask you to let him down lightly.'

With this subtle assumption of mutual paganism, he left finally.

'That is a worthy gentleman,' thought Manfred.

The chaplain was nervously anxious to secure an opening, and sought amidst the trivialities that led out of the conventional exchange of greetings a fissure for the insertion of a tactful inquiry.

Manfred, seeing his embarrassment, gave him the chance, and listened respectfully while the young man talked, earnestly, sincerely, manfully.

'N — no,' said the prisoner after a while, 'I don't think, Mr. Summers, that you and I hold very different opinions, if they were all reduced to questions of faith and appreciation of God's goodness — but I have got to a stage where I shrink from labelling my inmost beliefs with this or that creed, or circumscribing the boundless limits of my faith with words. I know you will forgive me and believe that I do not say this from any desire to hurt you, but I have reached, too, a phase of conviction where I am adamant to outside influence. For good or ill, I must stand by the conceptions that I have built out of my own life and its teachings.

'There is another, and a more practical reason,' he added, 'why I should not do you or any other chaplain the disservice of taking up your time — I have no intention of dying.'

With this, the young minister was forced to be content. He met Manfred frequently, talking of books and people and of strange religions.

To the warders and those about him,

Manfred was a source of constant wonder. He never wearied them with the recital of his coming attempt. Yet all that he said and did seemed founded on that one basic article of faith: I shall escape.

The governor took every precaution to guard against rescue. He applied for and secured reinforcements of warders, and Manfred, one morning at exercise seeing strange faces amongst his guards, bantered him with over-nervousness.

'Yes,' said the Major, 'I've doubled the staff. I'm taking you at your word, that is all — one must cling tight to the last lingering shreds of faith one has in mankind. You say that you're going to escape, and I believe you.' He thought a moment, 'I've studied you,' he added.

'Indeed?'

'Not here,' said the governor, comprehending the prison in a sweep of his hand, 'but outside — read about you and thought about you and a little dimly understood you — that makes me certain that you've got something at the back of your mind when you talk so easily of escape.'

Manfred nodded. He nodded many times thoughtfully, and felt a new interest in the bluff, brusque man.

'And whilst I'm doubling the guard and

that sort of thing, I know in my heart that that *something* of yours isn't *something* with dynamite in it, or *something* with brute force behind it, but it's *something* that's devilishly deep — that's how I read it.'

He jerked his head in farewell, and the cell door closed behind him with a great jangling and snapping of keys.

He might have been tried at the sessions following his committal, but the Crown applied for a postponement, and being informed and asked whether he would care to raise any objection to that course, he replied that so far from objecting, he was grateful, because his arrangements were not yet completed, and when they asked him, knowing that he had refused solicitor and counsel, what arrangements he referred to, he smiled enigmatically and they knew he was thinking of this wonderful plan of escape. That such persistent assurances of delivery should eventually reach the public through the public press was only to be expected, and although 'Manfred says he will escape from Wandsworth' in the *Megaphone* headline, became 'A prisoner's strange statement' in *The Times*, the substance of the story was the same, and you may be sure that it lost nothing in the telling. A Sunday journal, with a waning circulation, rallied on the discovery that Manfred was mad, and published a column-long account of this 'poor lunatic gibbering of freedom.'

Being allowed to read the newspapers, Manfred saw this, and it kept him amused for a whole day.

The warders in personal attendance on him were changed daily, he never had the same custodian twice till the governor saw a flaw in the method that allowed a warder with whom he was only slightly acquainted, and of whose integrity he was ignorant, to come into close contact with his prisoner. Particularly did this danger threaten from the new officers who had been drafted to Wandsworth to reinforce the staff, and the governor went to the other extreme, and two trusted men, who had grown old in the service, were chosen for permanent watch-dogs.

'You won't be able to have any more newspapers,' said the governor one morning. 'I've had orders from headquarters — there have been some suspicious-looking 'agonies' in the *Megaphone* this last day or so.'

'I did not insert them,' said Manfred, smiling.

'No — but you may have read them,' said the governor dryly.

'So I might have,' said the thoughtful Manfred.

'Did you?'

Manfred made no reply.

'I suppose that isn't a fair question,' said the governor cheerfully; 'anyhow, no more papers. You can have books — any books you wish within limits.'

So Manfred was denied the pleasure of reading the little paragraphs that described the movements and doings of the fashionable world. Just then these interested him more than the rest of the newspaper put together. Such news as he secured was of a negative kind and through the governor. 'Am I still mad?' he asked. 'No.'

'Was I born in Brittany — the son of humble parents?'

'No — there's another theory now.'

'Is my real name still supposed to be Isadore something-or-other?'

'You are now a member of a noble family, disappointed at an early age by a reigning princess,' said the governor impressively.

'How romantic!' said Manfred in hushed tones. The gravity of his years, that was beyond his years, fell away from him in that time of waiting. He became almost boyish again. He had a never-ending fund of humour that turned even the tremendous issues of his trial into subject-matter of amusement.

Armed with the authority of the Home

Secretary came Luigi Fressini, the youthful director of the Anthropological Institute of Rome.

Manfred agreed to see him and made him as welcome as the circumstances permitted. Fressini was a little impressed with his own importance, and had the professional manner strongly developed. He had a perky way of dropping his head on one side when he made observations, and reminded Manfred of a horse-dealer blessed with a little knowledge, but anxious to discover at all hazards the 'points' that fitted in with his preconceived theories. 'I would like to measure your head,' he said.

'I'm afraid I cannot oblige you,' said Manfred coolly; 'partly because I object to the annoyance of it, and partly because head-measuring in anthropology is as much out of date as bloodletting in surgery.'

The director was on his dignity.

'I'm afraid I cannot take lessons in the science — ' he began.

'Oh, yes, you can,' said Manfred, 'and you'd be a greater man if you did. As it is Antonio de Costa and Felix Hedeman are both beating you on your own ground — that monograph of yours on 'Cerebral Dynamics' was awful nonsense.'

Whereupon Fressini went very red and

167

spluttered and left the cell, afterwards in his indiscretion granting an interview to an evening newspaper, in the course of which he described Manfred as a typical homicide with those peculiarities of parietal development, that are invariably associated with cold-blooded murderers. For publishing what constituted a gross contempt of court, the newspaper was heavily fined, and at the instance of the British Government, Fressini was reprimanded, and eventually superseded by that very De Costa of whom Manfred spoke.

All these happenings formed the comedy of the long wait, and as to the tragedy, there was none.

A week before the trial Manfred, in the course of conversation, expressed a desire for a further supply of books.

'What do you want?' asked the governor, and prepared to take a note.

'Oh, anything,' said Manfred lazily — 'travel, biography, science, sport — anything new that's going.'

'I'll get you a list,' said the governor, who was not a booky man. 'The only travel books I know are those two new things, *Three Months in Morocco* and *Through the Ituri Forest*. One of them's by a new man, Theodore Max — do you know him?'

Manfred shook his head.

'But I'll try them,' he said.

'Isn't it about time you started to prepare your defence?' the governor asked gruffly.

'I have no defence to offer,' said Manfred, 'therefore no defence to prepare.'

The governor seemed vexed.

'Isn't life sufficiently sweet to you — to urge you to make an effort to save it?' he asked roughly, 'or are you going to give it up without a struggle?'

'I shall escape,' said Manfred again; 'aren't you tired of hearing me tell you why I make no effort to save myself?'

'When the newspapers start the *mad* theory again,' said the exasperated prison official, 'I shall feel most inclined to break the regulations and write a letter in support of the speculation.'

'Do,' said Manfred cheerfully, 'and tell them that I run round my cell on all fours biting visitors' legs.'

The next day the books arrived. The mysteries of the Ituri Forest remained mysteries, but *Three Months in Morocco* (big print, wide margins, 12s. 6d.) he read with avidity from cover to cover, notwithstanding the fact that the reviewers to a man condemned it as being the dullest book of the season. Which was an unkindly reflection upon the literary merits of its author, Leon Gonsalez, who had worked early and late to prepare the book for the press, writing far into the night, whilst Poiccart, sitting at the other side of the table, corrected the damp proofs as they came from the printer.

13

The Rational Faithers

In the handsomely furnished sitting-room of a West Kensington flat, Gonsalez and Poiccart sat over their post-prandial cigars, each busy with his own thoughts. Poiccart tossed his cigar into the fireplace and pulled out his polished briar and slowly charged it from a gigantic pouch. Leon watched him under half-closed lids, piecing together the scraps of information he had collected from his persistent observation.

'You are getting sentimental, my friend,' he said.

Poiccart looked up inquiringly.

'You were smoking one of George's cigars without realizing it. Halfway through the smoke you noticed the band had not been removed, so you go to tear it off. By the band you are informed that it is one of George's favourite cigars, and that starts a train of thought that makes the cigar distasteful to you, and you toss it away.'

Poiccart lit his pipe before replying.

'Spoken like a cheap little magazine

171

detective,' he said frankly. 'If you would know I was aware that it was George's, and from excess of loyalty I was trying to smoke it; halfway through I reluctantly concluded that friendship had its limits; it is you who are sentimental.'

Gonsalez closed his eyes and smiled. 'There's another review of your book in the Evening Mirror tonight,' Poiccart went on maliciously; 'have you seen it?'

The recumbent figure shook its head.

'It says,' the merciless Poiccart continued, 'that an author who can make Morocco as dull as you have done, would make — '

'Spare me,' murmured Gonsalez half asleep.

They sat for ten minutes, the tick-tick of the little clock on the mantelpiece and the regular puffs from Poiccart's pipe breaking the silence.

'It would seem to me,' said Gonsalez, speaking with closed eyes, 'that George is in the position of a master who has set his two pupils a difficult problem to solve, quite confident that, difficult as it is, they will surmount all obstacles and supply the solution.'

'I thought you were asleep,' said Poiccart.

'I was never more awake,' said Gonsalez calmly. 'I am only marshalling details. Do you know Mr. Peter Sweeney?'

'No,' said Poiccart.

'He's a member of the Borough Council of Chelmsford. A great and a good man.'

Poiccart made no response.

'He is also the head and front of the Rational Faith movement, of which you may have heard.'

'I haven't,' admitted Poiccart, stolid but interested.

'The Rational Faithers,' Gonsalez explained sleepily, 'are an offshoot of the New Unitarians, and the New Unitarians are a hotchpotch of people with grievances.'

Poiccart yawned.

'The Rational Faithers,' Gonsalez went on, 'have a mission in life, they have also a brass band, and a collection of drivelling songs, composed, printed and gratuitously distributed by Mr. Peter Sweeney, who is a man of substance.'

He was silent after this for quite a minute.

'A mission in life, and a nice loud brassy band — the members of which are paid monthly salaries — by Peter.'

Poiccart turned his head and regarded his friend curiously.

'What is all this about?' he asked.

'The Rational Faithers,' the monotonous Gonsalez continued, 'are the sort of people

173

who for all time have been in the eternal minority. They are against things, against public-houses, against music-halls, against meat eating, and vaccination — and capital punishment,' he repeated softly.

Poiccart waited.

'Years ago they were regarded as a nuisance — rowdies broke up their meetings; the police prosecuted them for obstruction, and some of them were sent to prison and came out again, being presented with newly furbished haloes at meat breakfasts — Peter presiding.

'Now they have lived down their persecutions — martyrdom is not to be so cheaply bought — they are an institution like the mechanical spinning jenny and fashionable socialism — which proves that if you go on doing things often enough and persistently, saying with a loud voice, '*pro bono publico*', people will take you at your own valuation, and will tolerate you.'

Poiccart was listening intently now.

'These people demonstrate — Peter is really well off, with heaps of slum property, and he has lured other wealthy ladies and gentlemen into the movement. They demonstrate on all occasions. They have chants — Peter calls them *chants*, and it is a nice distinction, stamping them as it does with the stamp of semi-secularity — for these festive moments, chants for the confusion of vaccinators, and eaters of beasts, and such. But of all their 'Services of Protest' none is more thorough, more beautifully complete, than that which is specially arranged to express their horror and abhorrence of capital punishment.'

His pause was so long that Poiccart interjected an impatient — 'Well?'

'I was trying to think of the chant,' said Leon thoughtfully. 'If I remember right one verse goes —

'*Come fight the gallant fight,*
'*This horror to undo;*
'*Two blacks will never make a white,*
'*Nor legal murder too.*

'The last line,' said Gonsalez tolerantly, 'is a trifle vague, but it conveys with delicate suggestion the underlying moral of the poem. There is another verse which has for the moment eluded me, but perhaps I shall think of it later.'

He sat up suddenly and leant over, dropping his hand on Poiccart's arm.

'When we were talking of — our plan the other day you spoke of our greatest danger, the one thing we could not avoid. Does it not seem to you that the Rational Faithers offer a solution with their querulous campaigns,

175

their demonstrations, their brassy brass band, and their preposterous chants?'

Poiccart pulled steadily at his pipe.

'You're a wonderful man, Leon,' he said.

Leon walked over to the cupboard, unlocked it, and drew out a big portfolio such as artists use to carry their drawings in. He untied the strings and turned over the loose pages. It was a collection that had cost the Four Just Men much time and a great deal of money.

'What are you going to do?' asked Poiccart, as the other, slipping off his coat and fixing his *pince-nez*, sat down before a big plan he had extracted from the portfolio. Leon took up a fine drawing-pen from the table, examined the nib with the eye of a skilled craftsman, and carefully uncorked a bottle of architect's ink.

'Have you ever felt a desire to draw imaginary islands?' he asked, 'naming your own bays, christening your capes, creating towns with a scratch of your pen, and raising up great mountains with herringbone strokes? Because I'm going to do something like that — I feel in that mood which in little boys is eloquently described as 'trying', and I have the inclination to annoy Scotland Yard.'

★　★　★

It was the day before the trial that Falmouth made the discovery. To be exact it was made for him. The keeper of a Gower Street boarding house reported that two mysterious men had engaged rooms. They came late at night with one portmanteau bearing divers foreign labels; they studiously kept their faces in the shadow, and the beard of one was obviously false. In addition to which they paid for their lodgings in advance, and that was the most damning circumstance of all. Imagine mine host, showing them to their rooms, palpitating with his tremendous suspicion, calling to the full upon his powers of simulation, ostentatiously nonchalant, and impatient to convey the news to the police-station round the corner. For one called the other Leon, and they spoke despairingly in stage whispers of 'poor Manfred.'

They went out together, saying they would return soon after midnight, ordering a fire for their bedroom, for the night was wet and chilly.

Half an hour later the full story was being told to Falmouth over the telephone.

'It's too good to be true,' was his comment, but gave orders. The hotel was well surrounded by midnight, but so skilfully that the casual passer-by would never have suspected it. At three in the morning, Falmouth decided that the men had been warned, and broke open their doors to search the rooms. The portmanteau was their sole find. A few articles of clothing, bearing the label of a Parisian tailor, was all they found till Falmouth, examining the bottom of the portmanteau, found that it was false.

'Hullo!' he said, and in the light of his discovery the exclamation was modest in its strength, for, neatly folded, and cunningly hidden, he came upon the plans. He gave them a rapid survey and whistled. Then he folded them up and put them carefully in his pocket.

'Keep the house under observation,' he ordered. 'I don't expect they'll return, but if they do, take 'em.'

Then he flew through the deserted streets as fast as a motor-car could carry him, and woke the chief commissioner from a sound sleep.

'What is it?' he asked as he led the detective to his study.

Falmouth showed him the plans.

The commissioner raised his eyebrows, and whistled.

'That's what I said,' confessed Falmouth.

The chief spread the plans upon the big table.

'Wandsworth, Pentonville and Reading,' said the commissioner, 'Plans, and remarkably good plans, of all three prisons.'

Falmouth indicated the writing in the cramped hand and the carefully ruled lines that had been drawn in red ink.

'Yes, I see them,' said the commissioner, and read '*Wall 3 feet thick — dynamite here, warder on duty here — can be shot from wall, distance to entrance to prison hall 25 feet; condemned cell here, walls 3 feet, one window, barred 10 feet 3 inches from ground.*'

'They've got the thing down very fine — what is this — Wandsworth?'

'It's the same with the others, sir,' said Falmouth. 'They've got distances, heights and posts worked out; they must have taken years to get this information.'

'One thing is evident,' said the commissioner; 'they'll do nothing until after the trial — all these plans have been drawn with the condemned cell as the point of objective.'

★ ★ ★

Next morning Manfred received a visit from Falmouth.

'I have to tell you, Mr. Manfred,' he said, 'that we have in our possession full details of your contemplated rescue.'

Manfred looked puzzled.

'Last night your two friends escaped by the skin of their teeth, leaving behind them elaborate plans — '

'In writing?' asked Manfred, with his quick smile.

'In writing,' said Falmouth solemnly. 'I think it is my duty to tell you this, because it seems that you are building too much upon what is practically an impossibility, an escape from gaol.'

'Yes,' answered Manfred absently, 'perhaps so — in writing I think you said.'

'Yes, the whole thing was worked out' — he thought he had said quite enough, and turned the subject. 'Don't you think you ought to change your mind and retain a lawyer?'

'I think you're right,' said Manfred slowly. 'Will you arrange for a member of some respectable firm of solicitors to see me?'

'Certainly,' said Falmouth, 'though you've left your defence — '

'Oh, it isn't my defence,' said Manfred cheerfully; 'only I think I ought to make a will.'

14

At the Old Bailey

They were privileged people who gained admission to the Old Bailey, people with tickets from sheriffs, reporters, great actors, and very successful authors. The early editions of the evening newspapers announced the arrival of these latter spectators. The crowd outside the court contented themselves with discussing the past and the probable future of the prisoner.

The Megaphone had scored heavily again, for it published *in extenso* the particulars of the prisoner's will. It referred to this in its editorial columns variously as 'An Astounding Document' and 'An Extraordinary Fragment'. It was remarkable alike for the amount bequeathed, and for the generosity of its legacies.

Nearly half a million was the sum disposed of, and of this the astonishing sum of £60,000 was bequeathed to 'the sect known as the Rational Faithers for the furtherance of their campaign against capital punishment,' a staggering legacy remembering that the Four Just Men knew only one punishment for the people who came under its ban.

'You want this kept quiet, of course,' said the lawyer when the will had been attested.

'Not a bit,' said Manfred; 'in fact I think you had better hand a copy to the *Megaphone*.'

'Are you serious?' asked the dumbfounded lawyer.

'Perfectly so,' said the other. 'Who knows,' he smiled, 'it might influence public opinion in — er — my favour.'

So the famous will became public property, and when Manfred, climbing the narrow wooden stairs that led to the dock of the Old Bailey, came before the crowded court, it was this latest freak of his that the humming court discussed.

'Silence!'

He looked round the big dock curiously, and when a warder pointed out the seat, he nodded, and sat down. He got up when the indictment was read.

'Are you guilty or not guilty?' he was asked, and replied briefly:

'I enter no plea.'

He was interested in the procedure. The scarlet-robed judge with his old, wise face and his quaint, detached air interested him mostly. The businesslike sheriffs in furs, the clergyman who sat with crossed legs, the triple row of wigged barristers, the slaving bench of reporters with their fierce whispers of instructions as they passed their copy to the waiting boys, and the strong force of police that held the court: they had all a special interest for him.

The leader for the Crown was a little man with a keen, strong face and a convincing dramatic delivery. He seemed to be possessed all the time with a desire to deal fairly with the issues, fairly to the Crown and fairly to the prisoner. He was not prepared, he said, to labour certain points which had been brought forward at the police-court inquiry, or to urge the jury that the accused man was wholly without redeeming qualities.

He would not even say that the man who had been killed, and with whose killing Manfred was charged, was a worthy or a desirable citizen of the country. Witnesses who had come forward to attest their knowledge of the deceased, were ominously silent on the point of his moral character. He was quite prepared to accept the statement he was a bad man, an evil influence on his associates, a corrupting influence on the young women whom he employed, a breaker of laws, a blackguard, a debauchee.

'But, gentlemen of the jury,' said the counsel impressively, 'a civilized community such as ours has accepted a system — intricate and imperfect though it may be — by which the wicked and the evil-minded are punished. Generation upon generation of wise law-givers have moulded and amended a scale of punishment to meet every known delinquency. It has established its system laboriously, making great national sacrifices for the principles that system involved. It has wrested with its life-blood the charters of a great liberty — the liberty of a law administered by its chosen officers and applied in the spirit of untainted equity.'

So he went on to speak of the Four Just Men who had founded a machinery for punishment, who had gone outside and had overridden the law; who had condemned and executed their judgment independent and in defiance of the established code.

'Again I say, that I will not commit myself to the statement that they punished unreasonably: that with the evidence against their victims, such as they possessed, the law officers of the Crown would have hesitated at initiating a prosecution. If it had pleased them to have taken an abstract view of this or that offence, and they had said this or that man is deserving of punishment, we, the representatives of the established law, could not have questioned for one moment the justice of their reasoning. But we have come into conflict on the question of the adequacy of punishment, and upon the more serious question of the right of the individual to inflict that punishment, which results in the appearance of this man in the dock on a charge of murder.'

Throughout the opening speech, Manfred leant forward, following the counsel's words.

Once or twice he nodded, as though he were in agreement with the speaker, and never once did he show sign of dissent.

The witnesses came in procession. The constable again, and the doctor, and the voluble man with the squint. As he finished with each, the counsel asked whether he had any question to put, but Manfred shook his head.

'Have you ever seen the accused before?' the judge asked the last witness.

'No, sar, I haf not,' said the witness emphatically, 'I haf not'ing to say against him.'

As he left the witness-box, he said audibly:

'There are anoder three yet — I haf no desire to die,' and amidst the laughter that followed this exhibition of caution, Manfred recalled him sharply.

'If you have no objection, my lord?' he said.

'None whatever,' replied the judge courteously.

'You have mentioned something about another three,' he said. 'Do you suggest that they have threatened you?'

'No, sar — no!' said the eager little man.

'I cannot examine counsel,' said Manfred, smiling; 'but I put it to him, that there has been no suggestion of intimidation of witnesses in this case.'

'None whatever,' counsel hastened to say; 'it is due to you to make that statement.'

'Against this man' — the prisoner pointed to the witness-box — 'we have nothing that would justify our action. He is a saccharine smuggler, and a dealer in stolen property — but the law will take care of him.'

'It's a lie,' said the little man in the box, white and shaking; 'it is libellous!'

Manfred smiled again and dismissed him with a wave of his hand.

The judge might have reproved the prisoner for his irrelevant accusation, but allowed the incident to pass.

The case for the prosecution was drawing to a close when an official of the court came to the judge's side and, bending down, began a whispered conversation with him.

As the final witness withdrew, the judge

announced an adjournment and the prosecuting counsel was summoned to his lordship's private room.

In the cells beneath the court, Manfred received a hint at what was coming and looked grave.

After the interval, the judge, on taking his seat, addressed the jury:

'In a case presenting the unusual features that characterize this,' he said, 'it is to be expected that there will occur incidents of an almost unprecedented nature. The circumstances under which evidence will be given now, are, however, not entirely without precedent.' He opened a thick law book before him at a place marked by a slip of paper. 'Here in the Queen against Forsythe, and earlier, the Queen against Berander, and earlier still and quoted in all these rulings, the King against Sir Thomas Mandory, we have parallel cases.' He closed the book.

'Although the accused has given no intimation of his desire to call witnesses on his behalf, a gentleman has volunteered his evidence. He desires that his name shall be withheld, and there are peculiar circumstances that compel me to grant his request. You may be assured, gentlemen of the jury, that I am satisfied both as to the identity of the witness, and that he is in every way worthy of credence.'

He nodded a signal to an officer, and through the judge's door to the witness box there walked a young man. He was dressed in a tightly fitting frock coat, and across the upper part of his face was a half mask.

He leant lightly over the rail, looking at Manfred with a little smile on his clean-cut mouth, and Manfred's eyes challenged him.

'You come to speak on behalf of the accused?' asked the judge.

'Yes, my lord.'

It was the next question that sent a gasp of surprise through the crowded court.

'You claim equal responsibility for his actions?'

'Yes, my lord!'

'You are, in fact, a member of the organization known as the Four Just Men?'

'I am.'

He spoke calmly, and the thrill that the confession produced, left him unmoved.

'You claim, too,' said the judge, consulting a paper before him, 'to have participated in their councils?'

'I claim that.'

There were long pauses between the questions, for the judge was checking the replies and counsel was writing busily.

'And you say you are in accord both with

their objects and their methods?'

'Absolutely.'

'You have helped carry out their judgment?'

'I have.'

'And have given it the seal of your approval?'

'Yes.'

'And you state that their judgments were animated with a high sense of their duty and responsibility to mankind?'

'Those were my words.'

'And that the men they killed were worthy of death?'

'Of that I am satisfied.'

'You state this as a result of your personal knowledge and investigation?'

'I state this from personal knowledge in two instances, and from the investigations of myself and the independent testimony of high legal authority.'

'Which brings me to my next question,' said the judge. 'Did you ever appoint a commission to investigate all the circumstances of the known cases in which the Four Just Men have been implicated?'

'I did.'

'Was it composed of a Chief Justice of a certain European State, and four eminent criminal lawyers?'

189

'It was.'

'And what you have said is the substance of the finding of that Commission?'

'Yes.'

The Judge nodded gravely and the public prosecutor rose to cross-examination.

'Before I ask you any question,' he said, 'I can only express myself as being in complete agreement with his lordship on the policy of allowing your identity to remain hidden.' The young man bowed.

'Now,' said the counsel, 'let me ask you this. How long have you been in association with the Four Just Men?'

'Six months,' said the other.

'So that really you are not in a position to give evidence regarding the merits of this case — which is five years old, remember.'

'Save from the evidence of the Commission.'

'Let me ask you this — but I must tell you that you need not answer unless you wish — are you satisfied that the Four Just Men were responsible for that tragedy?'

'I do not doubt it,' said the young man instantly.

'Would anything make you doubt it?'

'Yes,' said the witness smiling, 'if Manfred denied it, I should not only doubt it, but be firmly assured of his innocence.'

'You say you approve both of their methods and their objects?'

'Yes.'

'Let us suppose you were the head of a great business firm controlling a thousand workmen, with rules and regulations for their guidance and a scale of fines and punishments for the preservation of discipline. And suppose you found one of those workmen had set himself up as an arbiter of conduct, and had superimposed upon your rules a code of his own.'

'Well?'

'Well, what would be your attitude toward that man?'

'If the rules he initiated were wise and needful I would incorporate them in my code.'

'Let me put another case. Suppose you governed a territory, administering the laws — '

'I know what you are going to say,' interrupted the witness, 'and my answer is that the laws of a country are as so many closely-set palings erected for the benefit of the community. Yet try as you will, the interstices exist, and some men will go and come at their pleasure, squeezing through this fissure, or walking boldly through that gap.'

'And you would welcome an unofficial

form of justice that acted as a kind of moral stop-gap?'

'I would welcome clean justice.'

'If it were put to you as an abstract proposition, would you accept it?'

The young man paused before he replied.

'It is difficult to accommodate one's mind to the abstract, with such tangible evidence of the efficacy of the Four Just Men's system before one's eyes,' he said.

'Perhaps it is,' said the counsel, and signified that he had finished.

The witness hesitated before leaving the box, looking at the prisoner, but Manfred shook his head smilingly, and the straight slim figure of the young man passed out of court by the way he had come.

The unrestrained buzz of conversation that followed his departure was allowed to go unchecked as judge and counsel consulted earnestly across the bench.

Garrett, down amongst the journalists, put into words the vague thought that had been present in every mind in court.

'Do you notice, Jimmy,' he said to James Sinclair of the *Review*, 'how blessed unreal this trial is? Don't you miss the very essence of a murder trial, the mournfulness of it and the horror of it? Here's a feller been killed and not once has the prosecution talked about 'this poor man struck down in the prime of life' or said anything that made you look at the prisoner to see how he takes it. It's a philosophical discussion with a hanging at the end of it.'

'Sure,' said Jimmy.

'Because,' said Garrett, 'if they find him guilty, he's got to die. There's no doubt about that; if they don't hang him, *crack!* goes the British Constitution, the Magna Carta, the Diet of Worms, and a few other things that Bill Seddon was gassing about.'

His irreverent reference was to the prosecutor's opening speech. Now Sir William Seddon was on his feet again, beginning his closing address to the jury. He applied himself to the evidence that had been given, to the prisoner's refusal to call that evidence into question, and conventionally traced step by step the points that told against the man in the dock. He touched on the appearance of the masked figure in the witness-box. For what it was worth it deserved their consideration, but it did not affect the issue before the court. The jury were there to formulate a verdict in accordance with the law as it existed, not as if it did not exist at all, to apply the law, not to create it — that was their duty. The prisoner would be offered an opportunity to speak in his own defence.

Counsel for the Crown had waived his right to make the final address. They would, if he spoke, listen attentively to the prisoner, giving him the benefit of any doubt that might be present in their minds. But he could not see, he could not conceivably imagine, how the jury could return any but one verdict.

It seemed for a while that Manfred did not intend availing himself of the opportunity, for he made no sign, then he rose to his feet, and, resting his hands on the inkstand ledge before him:

'My lord,' he said, and turned apologetically to the jury, 'and gentlemen.'

The court was so still that he could hear the scratchings of the reporters' pens, and unexpected noises came from the street outside.

'I doubt either the wisdom or the value of speaking,' he said, 'not that I suggest that you have settled in your minds the question of my guilt without very excellent and convincing reasons.

'I am under an obligation to Counsel for the Treasury,' he bowed to the watchful prosecutor, 'because he spared me those banalities of speech which I feared would mar this trial. He did not attempt to whitewash the man we killed, or to exonerate him from his gross and sordid crimes. Rather, he made

194

plain the exact position of the law in relation to myself, and with all he said I am in complete agreement. The inequalities of the law are notorious, and I recognize the impossibility, as society is constituted, of amending the law so that crimes such as we have dealt with shall be punished as they deserve. I do not rail against the fate that sent me here. When I undertook my mission, I undertook it with my eyes open, for I, too,' he smiled at the upturned faces at the counsels' bench, 'I too am learned in the law — and other things.

'There are those who imagine that I am consumed with a burning desire to alter the laws of this country; that is not so. Set canons, inflexible in their construction, cannot be adapted according to the merits of a case, and particularly is this so when the very question of *merit* is a contentious point. The laws of England are good laws, wise and just and equitable. What other commendation is necessary than this one fact, that I recognize that my life is forfeit by those laws, and assent to the justice which condemns me?

'None the less, when I am free again,' he went on easily, 'I shall continue to merit your judgment because there is that within me, which shows clearly which way my path lies, and how best I may serve humanity. If you say that to choose a victim here and a victim there for condemnation, touching only the veriest fringe of the world of rascaldom, I am myself unjust — since I leave the many and punish the few — I answer that for every man we slew, a hundred turned at the terror of our name and walked straightly; that the example of one death saved thousands. And if you should seriously ask: Have you helped reform mankind, I answer as seriously — Yes.'

He talked all this time to the judge.

'It would be madness to expect a civilized country to revert to the barbarism of an age in which death was the penalty for every other crime, and I will not insult your intelligence by denying that such a return to the bad days was ever suggested by me. But there has come into existence a spurious form of humanitarianism, the exponents of which have, it would appear, lost their sense of proportion, and have promoted the *fear of pain* to a religion; who have forgotten that the Age of Reason is not yet, and that men who are animal in all but human semblance share the animal's obedience to corrective discipline, share too his blind fear of death — and are amenable to methods that threaten his comfort or his life.'

He flung out his hand toward the judge.

'You, my lord,' he cried, 'can you order the flogging of a brute who has half killed one of his fellows, without incurring the bleating wrath of men and women, who put everything before physical pain — honour, patriotism, justice? Can you sentence a man to death for a cruel murder without a thousand shrieking products of our time rushing hither and thither like ants, striving to secure his release? Without a chorus of pity — that was unexcited by the mangled victim of his ferocity? 'Killing, deliberate, wolfish killing by man,' say they in effect, 'is the act of God; but the legal punishment of death, is murder.' That is why I expect no sympathy for the methods the Four Just Men adopted. We represented a law — we executed expeditiously. We murdered if you like. In the spirit and the letter of the laws of England, we did murder. I acknowledge the justice of my condemnation. I do not desire to extenuate the circumstances of my crime. Yet none the less the act I cannot justify to your satisfaction I justify to my own.'

He sat down.

A barrister, leaning over the public prosecutor's back, asked:

'What do you think of that?'

Sir William shook his head.

'Bewildering,' he said in despair.

The judge's summing up was one of the briefest on record.

The jury had to satisfy their minds that the prisoner committed the crime with which he was charged, and must not trouble themselves with any other aspect of the case but that part plainly before them. Was the man in the dock responsible for the killing of Lipski?

Without leaving the box, the jury returned its verdict.

'Guilty!'

Those used to such scenes noticed that the judge in passing sentence of death omitted the striking and sombre words that usually accompany the last sentence of the law, and that he spoke, too, without emotion.

'Either he's going to get a reprieve or else the judge is certain he'll escape,' said Garrett, 'and the last explanation seems ridiculous.'

'By the way,' said his companion as they passed slowly with the crowd into the roadway, 'who was that swell that came late and sat on the bench?'

'That was his Highness the Prince of the Escorial,' said Charles, 'he's in London just now on his honeymoon.'

'I know all about that,' said Jimmy, 'but I heard him speaking to the sheriff just before we came out, and it struck me that I'd heard his voice before.'

'It seemed so to me,' said the discreet Charles — so discreet indeed that he never even suggested to his editor that the mysterious mask who gave evidence on behalf of George Manfred was none other than his Royal Highness.

15

Chelmsford

They took Manfred back to Wandsworth Gaol on the night of the trial. The governor, standing in the gloomy courtyard as the van drove in with its clanking escort, received him gravely.

'Is there anything you want?' he asked when he visited the cell that night.

'A cigar,' said Manfred, and the governor handed him the case. Manfred selected with care, the prison-master watching him wonderingly.

'You're an extraordinary man,' he said.

'And I need to be,' was the reply, 'for I have before me an ordeal which is only relieved of its gruesomeness by its uniqueness.'

'There will be a petition for reprieve, of course,' said the governor.

'Oh, I've killed that,' laughed Manfred, 'killed it with the icy blast of satire — although I trust I haven't discouraged the Rational Faithers for whom I have made such handsome posthumous provision.'

'You are an extraordinary man,' mused the

governor again. 'By the way, Manfred, what part does the lady play in your escape?'

'The lady?' Manfred was genuinely astonished.

'Yes, the woman who haunts the outside of this prison; a lady in black, and my chief warder tells me singularly beautiful.'

'Ah, the woman,' said Manfred, and his face clouded. 'I had hoped she had gone.'

He sat thinking.

'If she is a friend of yours, an interview would not be difficult to obtain,' said the governor.

'No, no, no,' said Manfred hastily, 'there must be no interview — at any rate here.'

The governor thought that the interview *here* was very unlikely, for the government had plans for the disposal of their prisoner, which he did not feel his duty to the State allowed him to communicate. He need not, had he known, have made a mystery of the scheme.

Manfred kicked off the clumsy shoes the prison authorities had provided him with — he had changed into convict dress on his return to the gaol — and laid himself down dressed as he was, pulling a blanket over him.

One of the watching warders suggested curtly that he should undress.

'It is hardly worth while,' he said, 'for so brief a time.'

They thought he was referring again to the escape, and marvelled a little at his madness. Three hours later when the governor came to the cell, they were dumbfounded at his knowledge.

'Sorry to disturb you,' said the Major, 'but you're to be transferred to another prison — why, you aren't undressed!'

'No,' said Manfred, lazily kicking off the cover, 'but I thought the transfer would be earlier.'

'How did you know?'

'About the transfer — oh, a little bird told me,' said the prisoner, stretching himself. 'Where is it to be — Pentonville?'

The governor looked at him a little strangely.

'No,' he said.

'Reading?'

'No,' said the governor shortly.

Manfred frowned.

'Wherever it is, I'm ready,' he said.

He nodded to the attendant warder as he left and took an informal but cheery farewell of the governor on the deserted railway station where a solitary engine with brake van attached stood waiting.

'A special, I perceive,' he said.

'Goodbye, Manfred,' said the governor and offered his hand.

Manfred did not take it — and the major flushed in the dark.

'I cannot take your hand,' said Manfred, 'for two reasons. The first is that your excellent chief warder has handcuffed me, behind — '

'Never mind about the other reason,' said the governor with a little laugh, and then as he squeezed the prisoner's arm he added, 'I don't wish the other man any harm, but if by chance that wonderful escape of yours materializes, I know a respected officer in the Prison Service who will not be heartbroken.'

Manfred nodded, and as he stepped into the train he said:

'That lady — if you see her, tell her I am gone.'

'I will — but I'm afraid I may not tell her where.'

'That is at your discretion,' said Manfred as the train moved off. The warders drew down the blinds, and Manfred composed himself to sleep.

* * *

He woke with the chief warder's hand on his arm and stepped out on to the platform as the day was breaking. His quick eye searched the advertisement boards on the station. He would have done this ordinarily, because they would tell him where he was, supposing for some reason the authorities had wished to keep his destination a secret from him. But he had a particular interest in advertising just then. The station was smothered with the bills of a travelling cheap jack — an unusual class of advertisement for the austere notice boards of a railway station. Huge flaming posters that said 'Everything is Right', and in smaller type underneath 'Up to-date.' Little bills that said, 'Write to your cousin in London . . . and tell her that Gipsy Jack's bargain,' etc. 'Go by the book!' said another. Marching down the stairs he observed opposite the station yet further evidence of this extravagant cheap jack's caprice, for there were big illuminated signs in evidence, all to the same effect.

In the shuttered darkness of the cab, Manfred smiled broadly. There was really no limit to the ingenuity of Leon Gonsalez. Next morning when the governor of Chelmsford Gaol visited him, Manfred expressed his intention of writing a letter to his cousin — in London.

★ ★ ★

'Did you see him?' asked Poiccart.

'Just a glimpse,' said Leon. He walked over

to the window of the room and looked out. Right in front of him rose the grim façade of the gaol. He walked back to the table and poured himself out a cup of tea. It was not yet six o'clock, but he had been up the greater part of the night.

'The Home Secretary,' he said between gasps as he drank the scalding hot liquid, 'is indiscreet in his correspondence and is generally a most careless man.' It was apropos of Manfred's coming.

'I have made two visits to the right honourable gentleman's house in this past fortnight, and I am bursting with startling intelligence. Do you know that Willington, the President of the Board of Trade, has had an affair, and that a junior Lord of the Admiralty drinks like a sponge, and the Chancellor hates the War Secretary, who will talk all the time, and — '

'Keeps a diary?' asked Poiccart, and the other nodded.

'A diary full of thousands of pounds' worth of gossip, locked with a sixpenny-ha'penny lock. His house is fitted with the Mag-no-Sellie system of burglar alarms, and he keeps three servants.'

'You are almost encyclopaedic,' said Poiccart.

'My dear Poiccart,' said Leon resentfully,

'you have got a trick of accepting the most wonderful information from me without paying me the due of adopting the following flattering attitudes: primary, incredulous surprise; secondary, ecstatic wonder; tertiary, admiration blended with awe.'

Poiccart laughed outright: an unusual circumstance.

'I have ceased to wonder at your cleverness, illustrious,' he said, speaking in Spanish, the language these two men invariably used when alone.

'All these things are beyond me,' Poiccart went on, 'yet no man can say for all my slow brain that I am a sluggard in action.'

Leon smiled.

★ ★ ★

The work of the last few weeks had fallen heavily on them both. It was no light task, the preparation of Three Months in Morocco. The first word of every seventh paragraph formed the message that he had to convey to Manfred — and it was a long message. There was the task of printing it, arranging the immediate publication, the placing of the book in the list, and generally thrusting it under the noses of an unappreciative public. As sailors store life-belts for possible contingencies, so, in every country had the Four Just Men stored the equipment of rescue against their need. Poiccart, paying many flying visits to the Midlands, brought back with him from time to time strange parts of machinery. The lighter he carried with his luggage, the heavier parts he smuggled into Chelmsford in a strongly-built motor-car.

The detached house facing the prison was fortunately for sale, and the agent who conducted the rapid negotiations that resulted in its transfer had let fall the information that the clients hoped to establish a garage on the Colchester Road that would secure a sensible proportion of the Essex motor traffic. The arrival of two rough-painted chassis supported this view of the new owners' business. They were enterprising people, these new arrivals, and it was an open secret 'on the road,' that Gipsy Jack, whose caravan was under distress, and in the hands of the bailiff, had found financial support at their hands. Albeit Jack protested vigorously at the ridiculous suggestion that he should open in Chelmsford at an unpropitious season, and sniffed contemptuously at the extravagant billing of the town. Nor did he approve of the wording of the posters, which struck him as being milder than the hilarious character of his business-entertainment called for.

★ ★ ★

'Them Heckfords are going to make a failure,' said Mr. Peter Sweeney in the bosom of his family. He occupied Faith Home, an ornate villa on the Colchester Road. Before his momentous conception of the Rational Faithers, it had borne the more imposing title of Palace Lodge, this by the way.

'They've got no business ability, and they're a bit gone on the sherbet.' For a high-priest of a new cult, Peter's language was neither pure nor refined. 'And they haven't got the common politeness of pigs,' he added ambiguously. 'I took the petition there today,' Peter went on indignantly, 'and the chap that come to the door! Oh, what a sight! Looked as if he'd been up all night, eyes red, face white, and all of a shake.'

' 'Good mornin', Mr. Heckford,' says I, 'I've come about the petition.'

' 'What petition?' says he.

' 'The petition for the poor creature now lyin' in Chelmsford,' says I, 'under sentence of death — which is legal murder,' I says.

' 'Go to the devil' he says; they were his exact words, 'Go to the devil.' I was that upset that I walked straight away from the door — he didn't even ask me in — an' just as I got to the bottom of the front garden, he

208

shouts, 'What do you want him reprieved for — hasn't he left you a pot of money?''

Mr. Peter Sweeney was very much agitated as he repeated this callous piece of cynicism.

'That idea,' said Peter solemnly and impressively, '*Must not be allowed to grow.*'

It was to give the lie to the wicked suggestion that Peter arranged his daily demonstration, from twelve to two. There had been such functions before, mass meetings with brass bands at the very prison gates, but they were feeble mothers' meetings compared to these demonstrations on behalf of Manfred.

The memory of the daily 'service' is too fresh in the minds of the public, and particularly the Chelmsford public, to need any description here. Crowds of three thousand people were the rule, and Peter's band blared incessantly, whilst Peter himself grew hoarse from the effect of railing his denunciation of the barbarous methods of a medieval system.

Heckford Brothers, the new motor-car firm, protested against the injury these daily paraders were inflicting on their business. That same dissipated man, looking more dissipated than ever, who had been so rude to him, called upon Peter and threatened him with injunctions. This merely had the effect of stiffening Peter Sweeney's back, and next day the meeting lasted three hours.

In the prison, the pandemonium that went on outside penetrated even to the seclusion of Manfred's cell, and he was satisfied.

The local police were loath to interfere — and reopen the desperate quarrel that had centred around such demonstrations before.

So Peter triumphed, and the crowd of idlers that flocked to the midday gathering grew in proportion as the interest in the condemned man's fate arose.

And the augmented band blared and the big drum boomed the louder and Rational Faith gained many new converts.

A sightseer, attracted by curiosity, was standing on the fringe of the crowd one day. He could not see the band from where he stood but he made a remarkable observation; it was nothing less than a gross reflection upon a valued member of the orchestra.

'That chap,' said this unknown critic, 'is beating out of time — or else there's two drums going.'

The man to whom he addressed his remarks listened attentively, and agreed.

The crowd had swayed back to the railings before the premises of the motor manufacturers, and as it dispersed — Peter's party 'processed' magnificently to the town before breaking up — one of the new tenants came to the door and stood, watching the melting crowd. He overheard this remark concerning the big drummer's time, and it vexed him. When he came back to the sitting-room, where a pallid Poiccart lay supinely on a couch, he said:

'We must be careful,' and repeated the conversation.

Until six o'clock these men rested — as men must rest who have been working under a monstrous pressure of air — then they went to clear away the results of their working.

At midnight they ceased, and washed away the stains of their labours.

'Luckily,' said Poiccart, 'we have many rooms to fill yet; the drawing-room can hold little more, the dining-room we need, the morning room is packed. We must start upstairs tomorrow.' As the work proceeded, the need for caution became more and more apparent; but no accident marred their progress, and three days before the date fixed for the execution, the two men, coming to their barely furnished living-room, looked at each other across the uncovered table that separated them, and sighed thankfully, for the work was almost finished.

'Those fellows,' said Mr. Peter Sweeney, 'are not so Bad as I thought they was. One of 'em come to me today and Apologized. He was lookin' better too, and offered to sign the petition.' Peter always gave you the impression in speaking that he was using words that began with capital letters.

'Pa,' said his son, who had a mind that dealt in material issues, 'what are you going to do with Manfred's money?'

His parent looked at him sternly.

'I shall Devote it to the Cause,' he said shortly.

'That's you, ain't it?' asserted the innocent child.

Peter disdained to answer.

'These young men,' he went on, 'might do worse than they have done. They are more business-like than I thought, darker, the town electrician, tells me that they had got a power current in their works, they have got a little gas-engine too, and from the way one of them was handling a big car today on the London road, it strikes me they know something about the business of motor-car running.'

★ ★ ★

Gonsalez, coming back from a trial trip on his noisy car, had to report a disquieting circumstance.

'She's here,' he said, as he was washing the

212

grime from his hands.

Poiccart looked up from his work — he was heating something in a I crucible over an electric stove.

'The Woman of Gratz?' he asked.

Leon nodded.

'That is natural,' Poiccart said, and went on with his experiment.

'She saw me,' said Leon calmly.

'Oh!' said the other, unconcerned. 'Manfred said — '

'That she would betray no more — I believe that, and George asked us to be good to her, that is a command.'

(There was a great deal more in Manfred's letter to 'his cousin in London' than met the governor's eye.)

'She is an unhappy woman,' said Gonsalez gravely; 'it was pitiable to see her at Wandsworth, where she stood day after day with those tragic eyes of hers on the ugly gate of the prison; here, with the result of her work in sight, she must be suffering the tortures of the damned.'

'Then tell her,' said Poiccart.

'That — '

'That George will escape.'

'I thought of that. I think George would wish it.'

'The Red Hundred has repudiated her,'

Leon went on. 'We were advised of that yesterday; I am not sure that she is not under sentence. You remember Herr Schmidt, he of the round face? It was he who denounced her.'

Poiccart nodded and looked up thoughtfully.

'Schmidt — Schmidt,' he puzzled. 'Oh yes — there is something against him, a cold-blooded murder, was it not?'

'Yes,' said Leon very quietly, and they did not speak again of Herr Schmidt of Prague. Poiccart was dipping thin glass rods into the seething, bubbling contents of the crucible, and Leon watched idly.

'Did she speak?' Poiccart asked after a long interval of silence.

'Yes.'

Another silence, and then Leon resumed:

'She was not sure of me — but I made her the sign of the Red Hundred. I could not speak to her in the open street. Falmouth's people were in all probability watching her day and night. You know the old glove trick for giving the hour of assignation. Drawing on the glove slowly and stopping to admire the fit of one, two, or three fingers . . . so I signalled to her to meet me in three hours' time.'

'Where?'

'At Wivenhoe — that was fairly simple too . . . imagine me leaning over the side of the car to demand of the willing bystanders how long it would take me to reach Wivenhoe — the last word loudly — would it take me three hours? Whilst they volunteered their counsel, I saw her signal of assent.'

Poiccart hummed as he worked.

'Well — are you going?' he asked.

'I am,' said the other, and looked at his watch.

★　★　★

After midnight, Poiccart, dozing in his chair, heard the splutter and the Gatling-gun explosions of the car as it turned into the extemporized garage.

'Well?' he asked as Leon entered.

'She's gone,' said Gonsalez with a sigh of relief. 'It was a difficult business, and I had to lie to her — we cannot afford the risk of betrayal. Like the remainder of the Red Hundred, she clings to the idea that we have thousands of people in our organization; she accepted my story of storming the prison with sheer brute force. She wanted to stay, but I told her that she would spoil everything — she leaves for the continent tomorrow.'

'She has no money, of course,' said

Poiccart with a yawn.

'None — the Red Hundred has stopped supplies — but I gave her — '

'Naturally,' said Poiccart.

'It was difficult to persuade her to take it; she was like a mad thing between her fear of George, her joy at the news I gave her — and remorse.

'I think,' he went on seriously, 'that she had an affection for George.'

Poiccart looked at him.

'You surprise me,' he said ironically, and went to bed.

Day found them working. There was machinery to be dismantled, a heavy open door to be fixed, new tires to be fitted to the big car. An hour before the midday demonstration came a knock at the outer door. Leon answered it and found a polite chauffeur. In the roadway stood a car with a solitary occupant.

The chauffeur wanted petrol; he had run himself dry. His master descended from the car and came forward to conduct the simple negotiation. He dismissed the mechanic with a word.

'There are one or two questions I would like to ask about my car,' he said distinctly.

'Come inside, sir,' said Leon, and ushered the man into the sitting-room.

He closed the door and turned on the fur-clad visitor.

'Why did you come?' he asked quickly; 'it is terribly dangerous — for you.'

'I know,' said the other easily, 'but I thought there might be something I could do — what is the plan?'

In a few words Leon told him, and the young man shivered.

'A gruesome experience for George,' he said.

'It's the only way,' replied Leon, 'and George has nerves like ice.'

'And after — you're leaving that to chance?'

'You mean where shall we make for — the sea, of course. There is a good road between here and Clacton, and the boat lies snug between there and Walton.'

'I see,' said the young man, and he made a suggestion.

'Excellent — but you?' said Leon.

'I shall be all right?' said the cheerful visitor.

'By the way, have you a telegraph map of this part of the world?'

Leon unlocked a drawer and took out a folded paper.

'If you would arrange that,' he said, 'I should be grateful.'

The man who called himself Courtlander marked the plan with a pencil.

'I have men who may be trusted to the very end,' he said. 'The wires shall be cut at eight o'clock, and Chelmsford shall be isolated from the world.'

Then, with a tin of petrol in his hand, he walked back to his car.

16

The Execution

If you pass through the little door that leads to the porter's lodge (the door will be locked and bolted behind you) your conductor will pass you through yet another door into a yard that is guarded by the ponderous doors of the prison at the one end and by a big steel gate at the other. Through this gate you reach another courtyard, and bearing to the right, you come to a flight of stone steps that bring you to the governor's tiny office. If you go straight along the narrow passage from which the office opens, descend a flight of stairs at the other end, through a well-guarded doorway, you come suddenly into the great hall of the prison. Here galleries run along both sides of the hall, and steel gangways and bridges span the width at intervals. Here, too, polished stairways criss-cross, and the white face of the two long walls of the hall are pitted with little black doors.

On the ground floor, the first cell on the right as you enter the hall from the governor's office is larger and more commodious than its fellows. There is, too, a suspicion of comfort in the strip of matting that covers the floor, in the naked gaslight which flares in its wire cage by day and night, in the table and chair, and the plain comfortable bed. This is the condemned cell. A dozen paces from its threshold is a door that leads to another part of the yard, and a dozen more paces along the flagged pathway brings you to a little unpretentious one-storeyed house without windows, and a doorway sufficiently wide to allow two men to pass abreast. There is a beam where a rope may be made fast, and a trapdoor, and a bricklined pit, coloured with a salmon-pink distemper.

From his cell, Manfred was an interested listener, as day by day the uproar of the demonstration before the gates increased.

He found in the doctor who visited him daily a gentleman of some wit. In a sense, he replaced the governor of Wandsworth as an intellectual companion, for the master of Chelmsford was a reserved man, impregnated with the traditions of the system. To the doctor, Manfred confided his private opinion of the Rational Faithers.

'But why on earth have you left them so much money?' asked the surprised medico.

'Because I dislike cranks and narrow,

foolish people most intensely,' was the cryptic reply.

'This Sweeney — ' he went on.

'How did you hear of Sweeney?' asked the doctor.

'Oh, one hears,' said Manfred carelessly. 'Sweeney had an international reputation; besides,' he added, not moving a muscle of his face, 'I know about everybody.'

'Me, for instance?' challenged the man of medicine.

'You,' repeated Manfred wisely. 'From the day you left Clifton to the day you married the youngest Miss Arbuckle of Chertsey.'

'Good Lord!' gasped the doctor.

'It isn't surprising, is it,' explained Manfred, 'that for quite a long time I have taken an interest in the various staffs of the prisons within reach of London?'

'I suppose it isn't,' said the other. Nonetheless he was impressed.

Manfred's life in Chelmsford differed in a very little degree from his life in Wandsworth.

The routine of prison life remained the same: the daily exercises, the punctilious visits of governor, doctor and chaplain.

On one point Manfred was firm. He would receive no spiritual ministrations, he would attend no service. He made his position clear to the scandalized chaplain.

'You do not know to what sect I am attached,' he said, 'because I have refused to give any information upon that point. I feel sure you have no desire to proselytize or convert me from my established beliefs.'

'What are your beliefs?' asked the chaplain.

'That,' said Manfred, 'is my own most secret knowledge, and which I do not intend sharing with any man.'

'But you cannot die like a heathen,' said the clergyman in horror.

'Point of view is everything,' was the calm rejoinder, 'and I am perfectly satisfied with the wholesomeness of my own; in addition to which,' he added, 'I am not going to die just yet, and being aware of this, I shrink from accepting from good men the sympathy and thought which I do not deserve.'

To the doctor he was a constant source of wonder, letting fall surprising items of news mysteriously acquired.

'Where he gets his information from, puzzles me, sir,' he confessed to the governor. 'The men who are guarding him — '

'Are above suspicion,' said the governor promptly.

'He gets no newspapers?'

'No, only the books he requires. He expressed a desire the other day for *Three Months in Morocco*, said he had half finished it when he was at Wandsworth, and wanted to read it again to 'make sure' — so I got it.'

Three days before the date fixed for the execution, the governor had informed Manfred that, despite the presentation of a petition, the Home Secretary saw no reason for advising the remission of the sentence.

'I never expected a reprieve,' he replied without emotion.

He spent much of his time chatting with the two warders. Strict sense of duty forced them to reply in monosyllables, but he interested them keenly with his talk of the strange places of the world. As far as they could, they helped him pass the time, and he appreciated their restricted tightness.

'You are named Perkins,' he said one day.

'Yes,' said the warder.

'And you're Franklin,' he said to the other, and the man replied in the affirmative. Manfred nodded.

'When I am at liberty,' he said, 'I will make you some recompense for your exemplary patience.'

At exercise on the Monday — Tuesday was the fatal day fixed by the High Sheriff — he saw a civilian walking in the yard and recognized him, and on his return to his cell he requested to see the governor.

'I would like to meet Mr. Jessen,' he said

when the officer came, and the governor demurred.

'Will you be good enough to refer my request to the Home Secretary by telegraph?' asked Manfred, and the governor promised that he would.

To his surprise, an immediate reply gave the necessary permission.

Jessen stepped into the cell and nodded pleasantly to the man who sat on the edge of the couch.

'I wanted to speak to you, Jessen,' Manfred said, and motioned him to a seat. 'I wanted to put the business of Starque right, once and for all.' Jessen smiled.

'That was all right — it was an order signed by the Czar and addressed personally to me — I could do no less than hang him,' he said.

'Yet you may think,' Manfred went on, 'that we took you for this work because — '

'I know why I was taken,' said the quiet Jessen. 'Starque and Francois were within the law, condemned by the law, and you strike only at those the law has missed.'

Then Manfred inquired after the Guild, and Jessen brightened.

'The Guild is flourishing,' he said cheerfully. 'I am now converting the luggage thieves — you know, the men who haunt railway stations.'

'Into — ?' asked the other.

'The real thing — the porters they sometimes impersonate,' said the enthusiast, and added dolefully, 'It's terribly uphill business though, getting characters for the men who want to go straight and have only a ticket of leave to identify them.' As he rose to go, Manfred shook hands.

'Don't lose heart,' he said.

'I shall see you again,' said Jessen, and Manfred smiled.

Again, if you grow weary of that repetition 'Manfred smiled,' remember that the two words best describe his attitude in those dreadful days in Chelmsford.

There was no trace of flippancy in his treatment of the oppressing situation. His demeanour on the occasions when he met the chaplain was one to which the most sensitive could take no exception, but the firmness was insuperable.

'It is impossible to do anything with him,' said the despairing minister. 'I am the veriest child in his hands. He makes me feel like a lay preacher interviewing Socrates.'

There was no precedent for the remarkable condition of affairs, and finally, at Manfred's request, it was decided to omit the ceremony of the religious service altogether.

In the afternoon, taking his exercise, he

lifted his eyes skyward, and the warders, following his gaze, saw in the air a great yellow kite, bearing a banner that advertised some brand or other of motor tires.

'Yellow kite, all right,' he improvised, and hummed a tune as he marched round the stone circle.

That night, after he had retired to rest, they took away his prison clothes and returned the suit in which he had been arrested. He thought he heard the measured tramping of feet as he dozed, and wondered if the government had increased the guard of the prison. Under his window the step of the sentry sounded brisker and heavier.

'Soldiers,' he guessed, and fell asleep.

He was accurate in his surmise. At the eleventh hour had arisen a fear of rescue, and half a battalion of guards had arrived by train in the night and held the prison.

The chaplain made his last effort, and received an unexpected rebuff, unexpected because of the startling warmth with which it was delivered.

'I refuse to see you,' stormed Manfred. It was the first exhibition of impatience he had shown.

'Have I not told you that I will not lend myself to the reduction of a sacred service to a farce? Can you not understand that I must have a very special reason for behaving as I do, or do you think I am a sullen boor rejecting your kindness out of pure perversity?'

'I did not know what to think,' said the chaplain sadly, and Manfred's voice softened as he replied:

'Reserve your judgement for a few hours — then you will know.'

* * *

The published accounts of that memorable morning are to the effect that Manfred ate very little, but the truth is that he partook of a hearty breakfast, saying, 'I have a long journey before me, and need my strength.'

At five minutes to eight a knot of journalists and warders assembled outside the cell door, a double line of warders formed across the yard, and the extended line of soldiers that circled the prison building stood to attention. At a minute to eight came Jessen with the straps of office in his hand. Then with the clock striking the hour, the governor beckoning Jessen, entered the cell. Simultaneously and in a dozen different parts of the country, the telegraph wires which connect Chelmsford with the rest of the world were cut.

It was a tragic procession, robbed a little of its horror by the absence of the priest, but sufficiently dreadful. Manfred, with strapped hands, followed the governor, a warder at each arm, and Jessen walking behind. They guided him to the little house without windows and stood him on a trap and drew back, leaving the rest to Jessen. Then, as Jessen put his hand to his pocket, Manfred spoke.

'Stand away for a moment,' he said; 'before the rope is on my neck I have something to say,' and Jessen stood back. 'It is,' said Manfred slowly, 'farewell!'

As he spoke he raised his voice, and Jessen stooped to pick up the coil of rope that dragged on the floor. Then without warning, before the rope was raised, or any man could touch him, the trap fell with a crash and Manfred shot out of sight.

Out of sight indeed, for from the pit poured up a dense volume of black smoke, that sent the men at the edge reeling and coughing backwards to the open air.

'What is it? What is it?' a frantic official struggled through the press at the door and shouted an order.

'Quick! the fire hose!'

The clanging of a bell sent the men to their stations. 'He is in the pit,' somebody cried, but a man came with a smoke helmet and went down the side. He was a long time gone, and when he returned he told his story incoherently.

'The bottom of the pit's been dug out — there's a passage below and a door — the smoke — I stopped that, it's a smoke cartridge!'

The chief warder whipped a revolver from his holster.

'This way,' he shouted, and went down the dangling rope hand over hand.

It was dark, but he felt his way; he slipped down the sharp declivity where the tunnel dipped beneath the prison wall and the men behind him sprawled after him. Then without warning he ran into an obstacle and went down bruised and shaken.

One of the last men down had brought a lamp, and the light of it came flickering along the uneven passage. The chief warder shouted for the man to hurry.

By the light he saw that what confronted him was a massive door made of unpainted deal and clamped with iron. A paper attracted his attention. It was fastened to the door, and he lifted the lantern to read it:

The tunnel beyond this point is mined.

That was all it said.

'Get back to the prison,' ordered the warder sharply. Mine or no mine, he would have gone on, but he saw that the door was well nigh impregnable.

He came back to the light stained with clay and sweating with his exertions.

'Gone!' he reported curtly; 'if we can get the men out on the roads and surround the town — '

'That has been done,' said the governor, 'but there's a crowd in front of the prison, and we've lost three minutes getting through.'

He had a grim sense of humour, this fierce silent old man, and he turned on the troubled chaplain.

'I should imagine that you know why he didn't want the service now?'

'I know,' said the minister simply, 'and knowing, I am grateful.'

★　★　★

Manfred felt himself caught in a net, deft hands loosened the straps at his wrists and lifted him to his feet. The place was filled with the pungent fumes of smoke.

'This way.'

Poiccart, going ahead, flashed the rays of his electric lamp over the floor. They took the slope with one flying leap, and stumbled forward as they landed; reaching the open door, they paused whilst Leon crashed it closed and slipped the steel bolts into their places.

Poiccart's lamp showed the smoothly cut sides of the tunnel, and at the other end they had to climb the debris of dismantled machinery.

'Not bad,' said Manfred, viewing the work critically. 'The Rational Faithers were useful,' he added. Leon nodded.

'But for their band you could have heard the drills working in the prison,' he said breathlessly.

Up a ladder at the end they raced, into the earth strewn dining-room, through the passage, inches thick with trodden clay.

Leon held the thick coat for him and he slipped into it. Poiccart started the motor.

'Right!' They were on the move thumping and jolting through a back lane that joined the main road five hundred yards below the prison.

Leon, looking back, saw the specks of scarlet struggling through the black crowds at the gates. 'Soldiers to hold the roads,' he said; 'we're just in time — let her rip, Poiccart.'

It was not until they struck the open country that Poiccart obeyed, and then the great racer leapt forward, and the rush of wind buffeted the men's faces with great soft blows.

Once in the loneliest part of the road they came upon telegraph wires that trailed in the hedge.

Leon's eyes danced at the sight of it.

'If they've cut the others, the chase is over,' he said; 'they'll have cars out in half an hour and be following us; we are pretty sure to attract attention, and they'll be able to trace us.'

Attract attention they certainly did, for leaving Colchester behind, they ran into a police trap, and a gesticulating constable signalled them to stop.

They left him behind in a thick cloud of dust. Keeping to the Clacton road, they had a clear run till they reached a deserted strip where a farm wagon had broken down and blocked all progress.

A grinning wagoner saw their embarrassment.

'You cairn't pass here, mister,' he said gleefully, 'and there ain't another road for two miles back.'

'Where are your horses?' asked Leon quickly.

'Back to farm,' grinned the man.

'Good,' said Leon. He looked round, there was nobody in sight.

'Go back there with the car,' he said, and signalled Poiccart to reverse the engine.

'What for?'

Leon was out of the car, walking with quick steps to the lumbering wreck in the road.

He stooped down, made a swift examination, and thrust something beneath the huge bulk. He lit a match, steadied the flame, and ran backward, clutching the slow-moving yokel and dragging him with him.

''Ere, wot's this?' demanded the man, but before he could reply there was a deafening crash, like a clap of thunder, and the air was filled with wreckage.

Leon made a second examination and called the car forward.

As he sprang into his seat he turned to the dazed rustic.

'Tell your master that I have taken the liberty of dynamiting his cart,' he said; and then, as the man made a movement as if to clutch his arm, Leon gave him a push which sent him flying, and the car jolted over the remainder of the wagon.

The car turned now in the direction of Walton, and after a short run, turned sharply toward the sea.

Twenty minutes later two cars thundered along the same road, stopping here and there for the chief warder to ask the question of the chance-met pedestrian.

They too swung round to the sea and followed the cliff road.

'Look!' said a man.

Right ahead, drawn up by the side of the road, was a car. It was empty.

They sprang out as they reached it — half a dozen warders from each car. They raced across the green turf till they came to the sheer edge of the cliff.

There was no sign of the fugitive.

The serene blue of sea was unbroken, save where, three miles away, a beautiful white steam yacht was putting out to sea.

Attracted by the appearance of the warders, a little crowd came round them.

'Yes,' said a wondering fisherman, 'I seed 'em, three of 'em went out in one of they motor boats that go like lightenin' — they're out o' sight by now.'

'What ship is that?' asked the chief warder quickly and pointed to the departing yacht.

The fisherman removed his pipe and answered: 'That's the Royal Yacht.'

'What Royal Yacht?'

'The Prince of the Escorials,' said the fisherman impressively.

The chief warder groaned.

'Well, they can't be on her!' he said.